Vibrashuns

Michael Savidge

Savidge Stories Press
Houston

Vibrashuns

This is a work of fiction. Names, characters, places, and incidents are either the product of the author's imagination or used fictitiously. Any resemblances to actual persons, living or dead, events or locales is entirely coincidental.

ISBN-979-8-9891145-0-4 Digital
ISBN-979-8-9891145-1-1 Hard Cover
ISBN-979-8-9891145-2-8 Trade Paper

Printed and bound in the U.S.A.
Book cover by oliviaprodesign.

Savidge Stories Press
Houston

Dedicated to my fascination with physics
and what could be….

Contents

Chapter 1 - Curious

Sitting on a stool in the local pub, I watched the people as I usually did on a Friday night. The patrons were all familiar, yet strangers to me as I had never taken the time to interact with them. My routine consisted of a few cold beers and maybe a shot or two of Crown, depending on my successes of the week. Working for a software troubleshooting firm had its perks. A drink or two on the company expense account was tolerated given my ability to bail one company after another out of trouble. A bit timid, I was left to my imaginings as to what each person or couple did and how they fit into the fabric of the scenes I portrayed them in.

I am a bit of a people watcher. Lurker is more like it. The more attractive ones would usually end up in a daydream or two. My bravado and charisma are legendary in my own mind. Getting them to be active participants in my imagination is easy.

Of late I had noticed a particular patron who had become a bit of secretive longing. I wished I had the social skills to approach her and start a dialogue at the very least. Watching her from the safety of my beer, I had witnessed a parade of men, and a few women, approach her, trying to engage her in conversation. She was polite and well-spoken but assured all who made the effort that she was not interested. To their dismay she dismissed their attempts at connecting as if to say, "does anyone possess an original bone in their body?"

She was a striking woman, perhaps 5 foot 7 or maybe 5 foot 8. Lightly tanned, she sat with an alert posture. This night, she was dressed in a simple pair of red slacks, a rose-colored shirt, and a black waist jacket. She looked great and the colors emphasized her beauty. Athletically built with proportionate breasts and long legs. Her hair was strawberry blond and looked like her natural color. Her neck was just long enough to be elegant, and her skin looked supple and smooth. I guessed her to be in her early forties, although she had the demeanor of someone with more vitality than her years suggested.

I sat puzzled and anxious. I'm fairly athletic and modestly attractive, just a touch over six feet tall and 185 pounds give or take a few. I've heard myself described as having rugged good looks. The proverbial five o'clock shadow is usually on my face by two p.m. A little dark complected, like I always have a nice tan. And I tend to the shy side.

My previous experiences with women, although not dismal failures, were certainly not memorable, nor had they lasted more than a couple of months. So how could I, with limited resources and modest social skills engage this striking woman before me? Perhaps the simple honest approach would be best. At the worst I would receive a slap across the cheek sending me back to the safety of my stool.

With a shot of Crown Reserve for courage and a quick spray of breath freshener, I gathered my wits and proceeded to the end of the bar where she sat. As I approached her, I realized she was not only striking, but also classically beautiful. This revelation did little to quiet my nerves. When I was within a few feet, she turned and casually took me in. Her deep green eyes were penetrating and for a moment took my breath away. There was a tenderness in her eyes that I had missed. It was as if I were seeing her for the first time. I paused mid-stride, reflecting for a second on my approach as I decided to stick with my gut.

"Hi, I'm Todd. Can I ask you a question?" I said. She paused, seeing something in my eyes that changed her demeanor ever so slightly. Perhaps it was hope that I would not spout some time worn expression in another attempt to engage her.

"Sure." she replied. "What's your question?"

"I've watched you for several months. I'm curious as to why you continue to come here. You seem to enjoy the atmosphere. Perhaps you like to watch people as I do. I find myself trying to guess what they do. The more attractive ones I include in some daydreams. Maybe you think like me?"

She smiled, "How refreshing to have someone recognize my zest for people watching and approach me with the same admission. Yes, I find it intriguing to guess what people do and engage them in fantasy roles. By the way, I'm Catherine."

My heart started to race. Had I met someone who shared my enthusiasm for fantasy? "May I join you?"

"Please do." she motioned to the stool next to her.

"I should be candid and tell you that I have you in some of my fantasies." I gave her a sly wink.

"Oh really, and just what are your intentions?" she winked back.

"I'd like to find a quiet place and get to know you better. Honestly, I'm a little shy and can't quite believe you're talking to me. I just couldn't sit on that stool any longer and not at least take a chance."

"Well, it's funny you should say that. I've been waiting patiently for you to make a move. As far as a quiet place goes, my home is a few short blocks away. Perhaps we should slip out."

For a moment I was stunned. Not in my wildest imaginings had I thought that my fantasies would come true. She looked at me as I tried to compose myself. I tried to be James Bond suave, to no avail. I was so nervous my knees were shaking under the camouflage of my trousers. We stood and came exhilaratingly close to each other. Her fragrance was subtle yet intoxicating. She came to me softly and wrapped her arms around me. The embrace was tender, but I could feel the raw power of her body beneath her dress. I instinctively returned her embrace and felt her shudder as my ever-swelling manhood pressed against her. Suddenly, my confidence returned.

As we left the pub, I could feel all eyes upon us. Some jealousy, some wonder. I knew that my stock had suddenly skyrocketed in that little Philadelphia pub.

The cool night air was refreshing, and I embraced the chill. Catherine shivered; I removed my coat and draped it over her shoulders. This brought a soft sigh of thanks to her lips.

We soon arrived at the stone stoop of a townhome. We were in an upscale part of Philly. Wrought iron railings guided us to the landing, and the door was an elegant expression in Honduran Mahogany. It appeared to be hand carved, hand waxed, not sealed in varnish, and very old. Ascending the few steps to the door she placed her hand on a small pad that looked like a stone, and the door quietly opened with a soft pop. Stepping into an expansive foyer, I was face to face with exquisite paintings. For a moment I wondered if they were prints, but upon closer inspection realized they were originals. Some were of obscure artists I had never heard of, and others were of notable fame. I recognized a Renoir, a Monet, and further down the hall saw what looked to be a Pollack. My time as a museum guard had paid off.

She draped my coat over a simple chair and came to me.

"I have been thinking of this moment for so long." Catherine said huskily.

She moved closer, and I took her in my arms and slowly kissed her. She parted her mouth slightly and my lips began a soft caress, a tender kiss at first, to taste her and feel the texture of her perfect lips. My tongue slowly began to explore her lips and mouth as she returned each movement. We moaned softly as the kiss grew in passion and intensity. We were lost in the moment as the simple act of kissing aroused us. We slowly parted, needing a moment to catch our breath.

"Mmm mmm." she whispered huskily. "Would you go to the study and pour us a drink while I inform the staff that I have a guest." She gestured to an open french door to her right.

"Sure." Staff? What, I wondered, had I gotten myself into? I saw an antique sideboard as I entered and moved towards it. The craftsmanship was superb. The piece looked to be a couple of hundred years old. Grasping the small brass handle, I raised the lid. An assortment of fine cordials presented themselves. Securing two glasses, I placed a few cubes of ice in each. I surveyed my choices. Choosing a premium bottle of bourbon, I poured two fingers in each glass. When I finished, she returned. Turning, I extended a glass towards her, which she softly took from my hand. Her hand brushed mine with an electric spark. I shuddered with anticipation.

"Ah, a Willet. One of my favorites. We are alone, as the staff has retired to their wing of the house. If there is anything you need, we can summon them. Would you like to take a tour of my home? Or we can begin to get to know each other a little better."

"I've thought about you for so long. I'd love to get to know you better. After that first kiss, I'm looking forward to the next one."

She gave me a long seductive gaze, as if she were making the last small commitment to our pleasure. With the speed and deftness of a Venetian pickpocket, she had my trousers unbuttoned, unzipped and around my feet.

She seemed amused that I hadn't worn any underwear. With a wicked smile, she grabbed my now aroused manhood. For a moment she performed a casual inspection, perhaps deciding how crazy she was going to make me.

"Relax your mind and body. Do not hesitate or hold back. Indulge yourself. Give in to the pleasure of this moment."

Not another word was spoken as she began her slow, sensual ministrations. This was totally new for me, as in my experience, women required that their needs be met before offering the mandatory "prize" as a small token of appreciation for my efforts. Not so with this incredible woman. I could see that she was truly enjoying herself. I began to slowly release my mind and body and allowed the divine sensations to wash over me. I felt waves of pleasure, slow at first, intensifying with each movement, one upon the other. She found erogenous zones I didn't even know I possessed and explored each enthusiastically.

I had no idea what she was doing, but never wanted it to stop. With a loud, deep moan, I felt an indescribable sensation of orgasmic pleasure such as I had never experienced.

I started to feel a bit dizzy and began to sag to the floor. She quickly grabbed a chair and slid it under me halting my descent. Exquisite aftershocks washed over my body, and I convulsed with little seizures of pleasure. I couldn't speak or stand. I was completely helpless and spent, not knowing when I might be able to move. I slowly began to calm down as she placed a cool towel over my forehead. I felt a warmness in my groin, and realized she was cleaning me with a warm towel. Exhausted, but with waves of endorphins washing through my body, I sat, happy for the first time in a long time. I was content and at peace with all around me. I was now indebted to this exhilarating woman for showing me a brief glimpse of pure heaven.

"Are you okay?" Catherine asked.

"I think so." was my weak reply.

"I was concerned for a moment. I thought you might pass out."

"It was close for a second there. I'm glad you found a chair." I chuckled.

"Catch your breath. I will be right back. But first …"

She bent over me, and I inhaled her sweetness. Her swollen lips pressed against mine, and I could taste a faint sweet, salty taste that must have been me. She gave me a soft, tender kiss and I could feel her quiver with a want not yet satisfied. Right then I had no clue as to how I would be able to reciprocate any time soon. She left, and I sat glowing as her steps faded.

It wasn't long before she returned with a tall glass of something, a smile and a wispy coral-colored teddy draped over her enticing figure.

"Wow, you look amazing."

"Thank you. My glass of cheer will rejuvenate you and allow us to continue our exploration."

"What is it?"

"This is part protein shake, part power shake with a variety of herbs to quickly rejuvenate your energy and fluids. It's Tim's special recipe. Tim is my butler, driver, and personal trainer among other things. We need to get you hydrated and at peak performance for what is to come."

I slowly drank the glass of fluid and was surprised at how good it tasted. It was thick and creamy like a shake but left none of the sugary residue in my throat. As I savored the last few drops, I began to feel a glow welling up from my midsection and washing over my entire body. It caught me a little off guard, as I wasn't expecting such immediate results. I started to feel an energy rush I hadn't experienced since my teens. Every fiber of my being felt energized and ready for anything.

As she stood there framed in the door of the study, she had let the teddy slip from her body. "Pretty amazing, isn't it? I just love the hint of cinnamon Tim puts in it. It reminds me of Christmas. Would you like to join me, au natural, for a tour of the house?"

I removed the rest of my clothing and was glad nature had provided me with a nice physique. Hitting the gym and martial arts twice a week helped, but mother nature had provided the basic structure. She turned to savor the sight of me, I felt the anticipation from her, the wanting to feel my body against hers. I was quickly recovering and even starting to swell a bit. She nodded approvingly and we headed for the kitchen.

As we walked, I noticed that I was not cold in the least. I realized the beautiful Italian marble floors were heated.

"Isn't it amazing that if your feet are warm, the rest of the body will follow. Mother Nature's thermostat."

"I feel great. That rejuvenated me faster than I thought possible. This is an incredible home. I could spend days just exploring each room."

"Thank you, Todd. Perhaps we can talk later about your request to stay a few days. But right now, I think we need to get to know each other a little better. Are you up for the challenge?"

"Yes." I replied huskily. I was incredibly turned on.

We entered a stunning kitchen. A Wolfe stove, Miele appliances, Sub Zero side-by-side fridge freezer, and beautiful distressed antique oak cabinets that had been hand rubbed to a soft tan luster. The countertops were of a material I had never seen. They looked like quartz but without the fracturing. The color resembled the sandy bottom of a mountain stream with traces of brown and red running through it. The faint streaks of color added to the overall effect of all the items in the room. It was a perfect blend of form and function.

As I turned to face Catherine, I paused, taking her in. It was one of those moments you never want to forget. There was so much strength in her movements, she had the suppleness of a giant cat. I realized that is what she reminded me of: a lioness on the prowl. She moved towards me with such grace and power that I was suddenly nervous that I might not live up to her expectations. Sensing my hesitation, she again encouraged me.

"Todd, relax. Allow yourself to embrace the novelty and wonder of our bodies. I promise you will be amazed at the heights of passion and joy you can experience."

I decided to heed her advice and approached her slowly. Her skin was smooth with light freckles here and there. She had fine downy hair all over her body, which gave her skin a texture that was soft to the touch. I started to kiss the nape of her neck slowly with small, soft kisses intended to arouse her. My left hand found her breast and she shuddered as I touched her. A soft moan escaped her lips. My lips traced their way to her mouth and started a slow, deep, passionate kiss. I could feel her respond; we were no longer two strangers sharing a moment of passion. We moved together in perfect unison as if we had always known each other. No stumbles or miscues, just sweet, passionate lovemaking. She moaned softly and pushed her hips toward me. I reached under her arms and lifted her up, gently placing her on the countertop. My face found its way down her breasts, across her tight washboard stomach, and nestled in her sweet center. It was so erotic to bring a woman to orgasm. I became enraptured with her pleasure. After exquisite minutes of oral indulgence, my aching erection longed to feel the inside of her. As I slid softly deep inside of her, a low, erotic groan escaped her lips. A beautiful rhythm ensued. Time stood still as we pleasured each other with the joy of new lovers. With wild abandon, we approached the climatic conclusion, and with loud primal screams, we slid quivering and smiling to the floor, unable to speak for a moment.

Finally, she said, “We will have to thank Tim for his magic elixir. Todd, you are amazing. My fantasies are now fueled by the reality that you can exceed my expectations. If you like I will call Tim and have him draw us a bath and serve us a small snack. Then we can retire until morning. I have a few things I would like to discuss with you. Are you able and willing to stay the night as my guest?"

How could I not respond in the affirmative? This was the most exciting experience of my life, and I didn't want the journey to end just yet.

"I would love to, Catherine."

With that said, we rose together. She made a quick call to Tim, grabbed my hand, and led me to what I hoped would be another adventure on a night already filled with more than I had dreamed of.

As we walked down the hall towards the master suite, I couldn't help but notice how big the townhome appeared to be. It didn't fit the dimensions of the outside, seeming much larger. We passed several doors on the way and eventually entered an octagonal foyer with double doors on three of the walls. Two walls were occupied by several chaise lounges and a Tiffany reading lamp. The opening to the foyer comprised the other three walls.

I felt like I was in a game show and wondered what was behind door number three.

When we approached the doors to the far left, they quietly opened. Stepping through, I let out a gasp as I took in the expanse of the bathroom. I lacked the words to properly describe what I saw.

"Catherine, I have been to several five-star resorts, and they pale in comparison to your bathroom."

"Thanks, Todd. It was a pleasure to create this space." she said with a light chuckle as she stood admiring her handiwork.

The room was enormous, probably twelve hundred square feet, all told. In the center was what appeared to be a small swimming pool. It was, in fact, the tub. I watched as she walked into the beach-like opening and sat on a ledge under the water. I followed slowly, trying to take in every detail in the room. The shape of the room was neither square nor rectangular, but more of a five-sided affair with alcoves on the outer walls. On one wall were conventional vanities and cabinets with bowl sinks. Another wall held a door that must have led to the water closet, where I'm sure the bidet and toilet resided. In the middle behind the tub was a glass block wall in the shape of a large conch shell. I assumed this was the shower.

Realizing that I was gawking, I moved to the entrance of the tub and began to walk down into the water.

"Mmmmm, that feels so good. The water is perfect."

"It does feel good. I like it at 96 degrees. You can stay in a bit and not raise your core temperature too much." she replied.

As I sat on the seat in the water, I looked up at the ceiling. The ceiling directly over the tub was domed, painted with a soothing cloud mural. A beautiful glass chandelier was suspended from the ceiling. If I did not miss my guess, it was a Murano.

With a quiet whoosh the doors opened and in walked a very attractive woman. She stood five foot five or six with long muscular legs and an athlete's physique. She was very full breasted. She had a European facial structure, and as she got closer, I could see her piercing green eyes. Beautiful auburn hair and darkly tanned skin.

Catherine smiled mischievously.

"Todd, this is Michelle LeFont. Michelle, this is our guest for the evening."

"So nice to meet you, Michelle." I said, blushing hard, as I realized I had stood up without thinking, and my attraction to her was in full view.

She let her eyes wander from my face to my knees and paused just long enough in the middle to produce a knowing, seductive grin.

"So very nice to meet you, Todd, I hope we become very close friends." she replied in a thick French accent.

"Todd, if you will allow Michelle to bathe you, I promise it will be an experience you won't soon forget." said Catherine.

Stammering a reply was not easy, as both women noticed my arousal.

"I see you shared one of Tim's secret concoctions, madam, oui?" giggled Michelle as she dropped her robe. I gasped, realizing that I had been doing a lot of that this evening. I felt a sudden wave of guilt as I realized I was staring and ignoring my host.

Sensing my discomfort, Catherine gently smiled.

"Todd, never be embarrassed about marveling at a woman's beauty. I find her as striking as you and would wonder if you failed to notice."

"I'm not used to such uninhibited behavior, and I'm struggling not to pinch myself or take my pulse."

Both laughed and it broke the tension, which was only coming from me.

Michelle walked towards me with the same grace and cat-like presence Catherine possessed. She poured some liquid soap into her hands. As she touched me, I shuddered as if an electric current had just run through me. Her hands were soft and supple. It was like a massage and bath at the same time. From my neck to my feet, she did not miss a spot. I hadn't realized that there were so many erogenous zones on my body. Under my arms, the small of my back, the back of my knees and even my wrists produced wave after wave of pleasure. I found myself floating somewhere between being conscious and unconscious. When she finished bathing me, I realized my eyes had been closed and that I had remained standing the whole time.

"Todd, may I pleasure you for a moment?" Michelle whispered in her soft, sultry French accent.

I glanced towards Catherine, and she nodded her approval. As Michelle moved me to the entrance of the tub I trembled in anticipation. When I lay down in the warm water, the surface under me was soft and pliable. Half of my body was out of the water, the other half warmed in the tub. Michelle knelt over me. "Très bon." she moaned as she slid softly onto me.

"May I join you two?" Catherine muttered huskily.

"Please." I replied, and the three of us began to enjoy an exquisite dance of lovemaking. As Michelle moved slowly up and down on my very aroused erection, Catherine lowered herself close to my lips that I might continue my exploration of her sweet center. Soon the eroticism was too much, and to my delight, I experienced another exquisite orgasm. Exhausted, I lay there taking in every delicious moment.

"I believe we need to feed him before we continue." Catherine laughed "Michelle, will you ring Tim and have him bring us some food?"

"Yes, madam."

Michelle walked over to a wall and opened the cabinet doors. Pulling open a drawer she produced three towels. To my surprise they were warm. Toweling dry with these two beautiful women was quite a treat as my mind was flooded with recent memories of naughty pleasures.

I heard a soft whoosh from the doors, as someone entered the room. I could only assume this was Tim. He looked average with brown hair and eyes. He was maybe 5 foot 10, around 170 pounds. He looked fit but not as athletic as the girls. You know that old saying, looks can be deceiving? He had that look.

"Hey guys, the food's in the other room waiting. I'll meet you there in a few minutes. I need to make Todd's new favorite drink. Right, Todd?" Tim said with a wink.

"Uh, yeah." I replied.

We walked over towards the towel cabinet and upon opening a cabinet door there was a small passage into another room. The room was done in a tropical set-ting with one wall entirely of glass looking out into an atrium. In front of the glass wall was a wrought iron table and chairs with a four-course breakfast sitting on the table.

"Everyone, take a seat and let's eat." Tim instructed. "I've got the juice."

The next hour was a blur, filled with small talk and great food. I was almost too exhausted to notice, but my favorite breakfast had been prepared for me. Now how did they know that?

Soon we went our separate ways. Catherine led me into a palatial master suite. As soon as my head hit the silk linens I was out. After all, it was almost five a.m., and I had to be at work at nine a.m. There was no way I was going to make it and I was too tired to care.

Chapter 2 – Proposal

My dreams were unusual and vibrant. In one of them I was a fifteenth century knight. It must have been the house, seeming like a castle to me. In the middle of a dream, I heard a sound that I hadn't heard before. As I slowly awoke, I realized I had been snoring. Was last night a dream? If it was, how do I keep it going, I wondered. Taking stock of my surroundings, I found myself in a huge king-sized bed, on silk linens after the best sex of my entire life. Yup, I'm dreaming, I decided.

A soft whirring noise pulled my eyes towards the windows. The draperies slowly parted, revealing a sunlit morning. And there was Tim, in desert fatigues and boots.

"Good morning, man. About time for you to crack out of bed, hit the deck and join us for breakfast." he said.

"What time is it?" I ask.

"Eleven hundred, for those of us who have served, eleven a.m. for everyone else." Tim replied. "There are clothes and toiletries laid out for you in the bathroom. Get cleaned up, enter the main hall, and make your way back to the kitchen area. We'll see you in a minute, daylights a burnin'." Tim quipped.

I was suddenly reminded of my days in the Army, and there was a familiar comfort I hadn't known I missed. "Yes sir." I replied. at your command."

He paused and gave me a look, neither friendly, nor curt, but there was steel in his gaze, and I realized he would be a formidable foe.

As I approached the table Catherine and Michelle turned and said good morning. Catherine looked ready for anything. She was in a black workout jumper. Michelle was dressed the same. After last night I found them both to be exotic. Wish I could think of a better word. Hot!!

Tim was at the stove, cooking a cheese and onion omelet, which is my second favorite meal.

"Who are you cooking that for?" I asked.

"For you, if you'd like one." Tim replied.

"Sounds great. Can I help?"

"No, I got it. You like hash browns, sliced tomatoes, and some fresh watermelon on the side."

"Amazing . . . but how do you know that?"

As I sat, the two women looked at me in slight amusement.

"What's so funny?"

"Todd, do you really think last night and today were pure chance?" replied Catherine.

For a moment I was stunned. This was a set-up? What possible reason could there be to involve me in anything? As I thought about it a little more, small pieces began to fit together, from her willingness to entertain me to her extraordinary staff, who apparently knew quite a bit about me.

"I'm not sure what you mean. Am I in danger of some sort? Is this a kidnapping with benefits? Please enlighten me."

Sitting casually across from me, Catherine looked at me and began. "Okay, a quick breakdown of your life, and then we will explain our position and our unique talents as they apply to you. Todd Peters; only son of William and Shirley Peters; both deceased. No living immediate family. Born 1981 in Portsmouth Virginia. Normal childhood, industrious youth, odd jobs here and there. Active in sports from seventh grade on. Had some close friends but did not stay connected to them. Graduated High School top ten percent of your class, mathematically gifted with an above average IQ. After one year of college, you dropped out. Joined the military, as an infantryman and enjoyed a memorable four-year career. You boxed as a light heavy weight for the Army and swam competitively for the post team in Korea. You were selected out of thousands of applicants to be on the Army pistol team. You trained with the Rangers and Special Forces. Your company In Fort Ord California made a trip to Coronado and enjoyed some close training with the Navy Seals. You applied for warrant officer testing, passed the tests, but had a small physical disability. As you were denied entrance into school, you opted to terminate service. You have been a carpenter, body shop repairman, a steel worker, and museum security guard, among other things. You earned your second-degree Black Belt in Choi Kwan Do. The last two years, after finishing trade school, you have been working for a computer programming firm as a troubleshooting technician. Unmarried, several relationships, but none moving forward. Does that about sum it up?" Catherine queried.

"That's accurate, but after hearing it in that manner it sounds disjointed and unfocused. I kind of feel like I may not have lived up to my potential. Such a short snapshot of me. Seems more memorable than how you've described it."

"Not at all. Your diversity of skills makes you the perfect candidate for what we have in mind. I will give you more information about my team as we go. All of them are hand-picked and have been trained in a variety of skills. We've tried to give them the tools they need to survive in today's world. I could not do without them. My last name is Bushnell, and yes that "Bushnell." My family made its fortune in optics, mostly lenses used in off world telescopes, and we continue to do well. I have taken an advisory position with the company to pursue other interests. We found recently that a lot of budding inventors/geniuses have gotten the short end of the stick, or had their inventions stolen from them. I believe something similar has happened to you?"

We were all sitting at the table, and Tim and Michelle seemed very interested in what Catherine had to say.

"Yea, I invented a portable fence, had it patented and had begun the process of finding a manufacturer when I realized it had been stolen and was already in production. I didn't have the resources to fight it."

"Well, in a nutshell, here is what we do: we find situations where someone needs help and come to their aid. We do, however, take on some formidable adversaries and have had our share of close calls. Your predecessor is no longer with us because of the events involved in a recent mission. Suffice it to say, he is alive and well, enjoying the rest of his life."

Wow, what have I gotten myself into? I mused.

"Of late, we have taken on more complex and dangerous projects. The one currently on the table is very dangerous and we believe what our client is working on could reshape the planet. We have been watching you for approximately two years. I know that sounds odd and may even shock you, but what we propose is very dangerous, very rewarding, and financially life altering."

"No way, I would have noticed." I shook my head.

"No offense, Todd, but you exist in what we call the white state. You are not always aware of your surroundings."

Just then a knife came whizzing by my head. Michelle reached out a hand, deftly catching it.

"What the hell" I exclaimed, jumping in my seat.

"Don't be alarmed. That was a small demonstration of what I just said to you. Tim threw the knife at you and Michelle caught it. You had no idea either event was going to happen, but my two teammates were prepared, as always. Do you now believe me a little bit?"

Angrily I replied, "Yes." I trembled a little. I couldn't tell if it was mostly fear or anger.

"Emotion is a great tool, if controlled. We have angered you because you feel threatened. You know from martial arts that this reaction is a flight or fight syndrome. When you can learn to harness that reaction and respond appropriately, then you become a tool to be reckoned with."

Suddenly I felt a little sheepish as I realized she was right. "I'm beginning to see your point."

"We, my team, and I, are not here to harm you. We wish to pull you into the fold and train you to help us prevent what could be an earth-altering event if the technology we hope to protect falls into the wrong hands. Have we gotten your interest?"

My heart raced, and I had the sudden urge to run. On one level I was terrified of these people, on another excited and calmed by their quiet assertiveness. Not sure what to say, I stammered, "Uh, Uh yes?"

"Fantastic. Then let's start with the basics. Catherine leaned forward across the table as if I would pay more attention that way.

"We called in sick for you. We would like you to break your lease and move into our home here. All your current financial obligations and debts will be eradicated, and you will fall off the grid. A new identity with history will be provided for you to help with concealment of all our efforts. Lastly, we will deposit 3 million dollars in a bank account of your choice, as a retainer. You will have access to the money after your training period is over. Obviously, your first order of business will be to disassociate yourself from any friends and quietly disappear. If you choose not to accept our offer, there will be no hard feelings. We can do a memory wipe of the last few days through a hypnosis technique made possible by one of the people we have helped and the brilliant technology they developed. Okay, crunch time. Are you in or out?" The three of them looked at me expectantly.

My mind was racing a million miles an hour. The money was preposterous, the timing incredible, as I was bored to tears with my life. The opportunity sounded exciting. For the first time in a great while, I was excited to be part of something greater than myself. Perhaps this was the moment/situation I had been looking for. As I looked at each of them in turn, I detected no judgement. They were waiting for my reply.

"Catherine, I'm in, and I'll do my best not to let you down."

With a blur of movement, Tim expertly put me in a rear naked choke with perfect precision. Instinctively, I turned my head into the crook of his arm and kicked my chair back as hard as I could. As I did, I slumped towards the ground and grabbed his leading leg. I could feel the enormous pressure I was putting on his now hyper-extended knee. He softened his grip for a moment. As he did, I shot my arm between his arm and my neck, turning towards his lead leg to break his grip. Realizing that his knee was going to break, he let go and I spun into a crouch. I felt prepared for anything.

"Pretty cool, Todd. For the first time since we have been watching you, your instincts took over, and you were in an Orange State of awareness. No more for now, so just relax."

"Are you okay Tim?"

"Yeah, I'm fine." he said as he rolled his knee around to loosen it up.

"Interesting defense for a rear, naked choke hold. Is that something from an instructor or was it instinct?" Tim asked as he stretched his leg out.

"I didn't think. I just reacted."

"He is going to be just fine, Cat. You were right on the money about this guy."

"Let's all break for a while", said Catherine. "I will show Todd our facilities. We will see everyone at two p.m. in the upstairs training room. Until then."

Catherine gave me an amused glance as she explained the layout of her home. “I suppose you are a bit confused as to how so much is crammed into what would seem a simple Philadelphian townhome on Lombard Street?”

“I am. It just doesn’t fit with the space from the outside. I replied in a puzzled tone.”

“Consider this, then. If you were to take two townhomes on this street and two townhomes on the street behind us, would that make more sense?” she said as we walked towards the rear of the home.

“Yes, it would.”

“Well, that is exactly what we’ve done. I purchased four townhomes backing up to each other and made them into one unit. We have around fifteen thousand square feet, plus the garages. A full gymnasium, shooting range, and technical areas are encompassed into this home, along with sleeping areas and leisure spaces. Two of the townhomes have two-story basements. These areas are for the shooting range and the garages. We have a wide assortment of vehicles and the finest surveillance equipment we could find. We have several contracts with satellite companies and can access real-time situations almost anywhere in the world. As we go through your training, you will become more familiar with the layout of this facility and its unique capabilities to assist us in our endeavors. For now, I wish to show you the garage and shooting range as they are perhaps the cleverest part of this home."

"I'm impressed by the effort it must have taken to put this all together. How you did it all with no one the wiser is beyond me."

We came to what I thought was the middle of the house. Catherine opened an exquisite antique cabinet. Inside was a small hall and at the end a stainless-steel wall. She walked up to the wall and put her right hand against it. A pleasant feminine South African accented voice spoke softly. "Good morning, Catherine. What floor would you like to access?"

"Subterranean level two, please. Todd, I would like you to meet Elle. She is the avatar of our computer system. Elle, this is Todd Peters."

"Pleased to meet you, Todd." Elle replied as a small wand extended from the wall. A bluish light emanated from the wand and slid up and down the length of Catherine, inches from her body.

"DNA scan complete. Would you like me to archive Todd at this time?" said Elle.

"Yes, please. Todd, stand where I stood, and the machine will take a DNA sampling of you. The device takes a sample from different areas of your body. Another gadget from a previous inventor we helped. It's a shame so many good people with great ideas get swindled or taken for all their effort. We try to mitigate those circumstances where we can. It's harmless, as the machine reads the microscopic dust or dead skin that flakes off your body every second. It is impossible to imitate and allows only a chosen few to access restricted areas. Last chance to turn back." My sultry host looked searchingly into my eyes.

"No, you have my undivided attention." I asserted.

It felt like I was a novice entering a high stakes poker game. Some part of me was blossoming, and this excited me. I could not wait for the next discovery. As the wand scanned me, I thought of the person who developed this device. How cool to be able to read a speck of dead skin floating in the air and immediately identify the host.

“Scan complete. Todd Peters is now on file and archived into all current databases. Will there be anything else, Catherine?”

“That’s all for now.”

With no other fanfare the seemingly stainless-steel wall visually disappeared, and a cargo elevator stood ready for occupancy. “The wall is a holograph?” I asked, amazed.

“Yes, the technology it takes to produce a holograph of this clarity is extraordinary.” said Catherine.

As we entered the platform the wall reappeared, and I couldn’t see where we had come from. With no noise, the elevator began a quick descent. As we descended, I could see the structure of the elevator shaft. It looked like we moved about fifty feet.

When we softly touched down, the holograph shielding the opening disappeared. Before me was the garage area. I was blown away by the variety and sheer number of vehicles on the floor. Most were stacked two high on lifts. There was even a Prevost motor home on the far wall. I'm sure my mouth was open, and I was gawking.

"This is impressive. Can't wait for you to show me around." I said as we stood just outside the elevator.

"That's why we are here, my new protégé." she said with a sense of pride. "As you can see, we have a variety of vehicles, some plain, others exotic, some utilitarian, and some job specific. We have several garages scattered around the world with cars that fit the style of the country they are in. Each garage is part of a retreat or a safe house where we can rest, seek medical or technological help, or renew assets and weaponry. Each retreat contains the same technology as the home we are in. Most of them are fireproof and virtually impossible to breach short of an all-out assault."

As we walked into the main area Catherine continued, "We place some of them in urban areas and some in rural areas in order to meet our requirements. We have two private jets, one on each coast and several yachts scattered around in different ports or harbors. All in all, we are extraordinarily well prepared to help other people, and protect our assets and ourselves. Any questions yet?"

"I'm overwhelmed. You read about organizations like this in a novel, but never suspect they really exist." I said with wonder and admiration.

"For organizations such as ours, there is a counter group of equal or greater strength. Our choice is to help people, but I can assure you, as passionate as we are about what we do, our adversaries are equally passionate, and will risk everything to achieve their goals."

"I completely believe you. I can see that you go to great lengths to give people the tools to succeed."

"Let's go up one level to the shooting range. We will revisit the garage when the driving portion of your training begins." she suggested while we walked back towards the blank stainless-steel wall to the concealed elevator.

As we exited the elevator and walked into the room, I suddenly felt like a ten-year-old with a Daddy Warbucks American Express card, on the shopping trip of a lifetime.

My first impression of the "range" was of something I thought you would see at a Langley training facility. I'm a gun guy, and I love weapons of all sorts from the very primitive to high tech. I think all weapons have a time and place and serve the purpose they were intended for. Some can be multifunctional, serving a variety of uses. When I saw the arsenal before me, I was stunned. There was everything from a 14th century broad axe to something that looked as if it was directly out of a science fiction movie.

"Quite the selection, isn't it?" Catherine said.

"Pretty diverse selection of weaponry, and I am stoked with anticipation. I can't wait to get my hands on some of those weapons." was my excited reply.

Outside of the immediate cache area of weapons was a bench area for sighting, and targets for posture firing. To the left of this were rural and urban landscapes with pop up targets scattered around. I guessed this was for dry mission runs and target identification and acquisition.

"Tim is very proficient in all the weaponry here and will be your primary instructor. Michelle will be your close combat and etiquette instructor, and I will handle all your demolition training."

"I can hardly wait."

With an agility I did not know she possessed, she suddenly leapt forward in a classic side-kick pose. Without thinking, I opened my body to the left and gathered her in my arms as she slid silently by. Immediately I placed a passionate kiss on her eager lips and felt myself begin to stiffen. She moaned softly as I felt the tension drain from her.

"Nice catch." she softly replied as she enthusiastically returned my kiss. When we separated, I set her on the ground and she said, "Let's go to the conference room for our meeting with the team."

"I would enjoy being with you again, Catherine. May I call you Cat?"

"If you promise to repeat your first performance, I think we can work something in." she laughed, "But first let's get you trained up. If you have any energy left, then we'll see." she said with a grin.

Chapter 3 – Training

As we approached the elevator Elle asked, "What floor would you like, Catherine?"

"Fifth floor, please."

We stepped off the elevator to a room paneled with Honduran mahogany, and floors covered in walnut planking of various widths. A conference table that appeared to be suspended in midair occupied the center of the room. Overhead was a beautiful arrangement of old wood beams and glass panels, letting in the maximum amount of light. This produced a softness to the atmosphere that did not escape me.

"Yo, Todd, pretty cool, right?" quipped Tim as he turned to greet us dressed in what looked like Navy fatigues. He was a striking figure. The more I saw of him the more my instinctive respect for him grew.

"The whole place is cool. Each floor gives me a new perspective on your level of commitment and preparedness." was my reply.

As I approached the table. I could see the chairs were comfortable looking. The table still had me confused on how it just hung there. Hopefully, I will get a chance to find out.

"Let's all be seated, and we can begin." directed Catherine.

"Todd, sit here, please, and we will start your introduction. Let me begin by saying we are glad you made the decision to become part of the team. Your life will never be the same. Your training will take approximately six months. We would usually take a full year, but our timetable just won't allow the extra time. Your training will be extensive. You will train twenty-four hours a day, seven days a week. As you sleep some interesting things will happen. Acquiring ground-breaking technology from those we help has its advantages. We are in possession of a device that helps rewrite and overwrite your neural pathways. When you wake each morning, you will have a working knowledge of the skills you will need for the day's lessons. As your mind becomes accustomed to receiving the new instructions from what the team has affectionately named Nimmrod, which stands for Neural Implant Muscle Memory Redirecting Osmatic Device, you will acquire new skill levels that will seem almost unrealistic. How can your mind learn to do new things while you sleep? How can your muscles and nerves learn to perform in ways you are not used to?" she asked rhetorically.

"That is what this device does. Makes the seemingly impossible, possible. Your body will move differently. Your mind will think more clearly, and your problem-solving skills will quicken. Your brain's ability to assimilate information is only limited by your neural receptors, some proteins, and the order in which they respond. We are going to kick your brain into hyper drive."

"Are there any downsides or side effects?" I asked nervously.

"Yeah, you become a smart-ass-know-it-all overnight." said Tim.

This brought a chuckle from everyone.

"There are a few. The most noticeable is a feeling of exhaustion as your brain will be working 24/7. Hence, the lovely concoction Tim makes for us daily. There are a few other proteins and some genetic shakes we would like you to take, which speed up the recovery period. They also help the new brain tissue hold and retain the knowledge we are pumping into it. When the six-month training is finished, you will have comprehensive knowledge from the teachings of the Bible to the skill sets necessary to land a stealth jet on an aircraft carrier at night. With that said, let us dim the lights, darken the glass above, drop the screen, and get started." she leaned forward as if to emphasize every word.

"Let's talk about assets. Most often, an asset refers to a person or persons, able to facilitate a mission's success, whether they know it or not. There are also mechanical and biological assets that we will discuss later. We use people to our advantage. Some are awarded monetary compensation; others do it for the rightness of it all, and some never know they have been used. The unfortunate aspect of an asset is sometimes they become victims of collateral damage. That is never our intention, and we go to great lengths to prevent it from happening. But it does happen. The first and most important lesson is to never allow an asset to redirect the operation or to affect your ability to perform effectively and complete the mission. The greater good will always prevail, and everyone's journey through life is their own. Sounds trite, I know, but think about it for a moment. You have no more control of a squirrel being hit by a passing car than you do of affecting lasting change in an individual's life journey. Remember this and own it. It can potentially save your life and those of the team.

"Next, never underestimate a situation, locale or an adversary. Every moment is an opportunity to create a new pathway in the fabric of time. Seize each moment and endeavor to prevail.

"Then there are tools. All things are tools, from a kitchen knife to a stealth fighter. Learn to respect their individual complexities and embrace their ability to protect and serve the mission as it applies to the situation.

"Next is money, which is one of the most powerful tools in our possession. Most things can be streamlined and made relatively effortless if monetary leverage is applied in the correct areas. Be it known that we are not, nor ever will be short of money. Use it wisely and watch how effective you can be. Use it poorly, and you risk all. People are greedy by nature and will attempt to exploit you as often as possible. Any questions, Todd?"

"A few, but they can wait."

This was interesting and a little dark all at the same time. I wasn't sure if I liked it. but I respected what she was telling me.

"We would prefer that you ask them now. Remember, the poor question is the one not asked, as it gives only you a perspective on your misgivings or inability to form a proper plan."

"What if a family member were to become an asset, or if you inadvertently involved someone and realized they were in way over their heads?"

"That is the primary reason we search for team members with small or no family ties. You become a larger target when an adversary realizes they can exact changes in your actions by exerting pressure on a loved one or family member. You will involve people to help you from time to time that are not capable. Become a student of human nature and learn to identify the qualities in an asset that will prevail. As you progress, your errors will diminish, and you will become proficient at recruiting quality assets."

"I see your point. Sounds a little cutthroat, but I suppose the stakes are so high that it needs to be that way." Again, that uneasiness crept in. I wondered if I was in over my head. I guessed time would tell. I hoped the knot in my stomach would go away soon. Maybe I was hungry. Ha!

The next few hours were a blur. We talked about so many topics, I felt like I didn't have a chance of remembering half of them. Before we knew it, it was seven thirty. Everyone looked a little beat. I know I was.

"Let's break for dinner. We will reconvene in the Suit room and get our new teammate fitted for his Nimmrod adventure."

"Hey Todd, do you like pizza?" Tim asked.

"Yeah, love it, is that what's for dinner?" I replied.

"Yeah, we are human too, brother. A good Chicago style pizza pie with a nice Bordeaux would be great. Michelle and I will head to the kitchen."

"Todd and I will be down in a moment." Catherine looked at me and asked, "How are you holding up? It's a lot to absorb in such a short time frame. The Suit will help immensely."

"It's a lot to take in. I find it hard to believe I was scouted for two years and I'm part of something you see at the movies or read in a techno thriller."

"The things you will see, and experience will amaze you, I promise. Your life is about to change forever, and you will go out into the world with a perspective and knowledge few ever achieve."

Dinner was great. The pizza was extraordinary and the wine superb.

"Do we have a wine cellar?" I queried.

"Oui, we do. For the first time you spoke as one of the team." Michelle exclaimed. "I will show you the cellar later as one of your lessons. We will sample a variety of wines. I can teach you the art of drinking fine wines. Perhaps we will have time to continue the conversation that we started in the tub, no?"

"Well, both of those adventures sound inviting to me. I love a good wine and have some experience in the procurement and tasting of finer wines." I grinned.

With a wave of her hand, Michelle left the table and headed for the elevator. "See everyone in the Suit room. I will go get everything ready."

"Thanks, Michelle. We will see you in a moment" Catherine responded. "Tim, can you show Todd to the room, and I will be along. Get him fitted. I will see all of you in a few minutes."

"You got it Cat." Tim said. "C'mon stud, you're gonna' freak out on this. Prepare to enter a world of capabilities less than one tenth of one percent of the human race ever even gets close to. Yeah, baby, you're gonna' have the ride of your life." he said with a look of amusement, or glee, I wasn't sure which.

Again, I wondered what the hell I had gotten myself into.

We entered the Suit room through an airlock with a set of glass doors. I could see Michelle already inside dressed in a white surgical smock that covered her from head to toe. She had on surgical slippers and a mask that looked like a small version of a respirator.

As the door shut behind us Tim spoke. "Okay, man, off with the clothes, and walk into the shower enclosure. The door will seal behind you. A combination of lasers and airborne chemicals will cover every inch of you. Keep your eyes open for as long as you can. The laser is a cold laser that will help exfoliate your skin and will feel like you're getting a mild sunburn. The chemicals temporarily slow the growth and reproduction of your skin's bacteria. We need good contact between you and the suit. In you go, try to relax. It takes about three minutes. As soon as you see the green light, enter the room where Michelle is, and she'll tell you what to do next. I'll be in the outside room at the control panel."

The sensation of the laser was pleasant. I could feel it scrubbing the old skin away, with every wisp of air and every molecule that touched it. Freaky and cool at the same time.

"Breathe, man, jeez, dang newbies. Tim chuckled as I realized I had been holding my breath. Inside the room I could see a screen behind Michelle that displayed all my body functions, from heart rate to blood pressure to respiration. I wondered how they did that. As far as I could tell, I wasn't hooked to any device.

"The shower is the device. It is monitoring you as it performs. Kinda cool, right?" remarked Tim, reading my thoughts.

With an amazed look on my face, I spoke. "Hard to believe I've never seen any of this technology before, since that's what I've been doing for the last couple of years, military grade technology support and repair."

"Well, this stuff we have is beyond military grade. These devices are so cutting edge that few people have ever seen them, let alone used them. We hope to change all that. All right, you're done. Walk into the room where Michelle is."

I swear I could feel every molecule in the room as it met my skin. A smile broke out on my lips, as I found the sensation quite pleasurable. It felt better than stepping into a hot shower after a hard workout or a long day.

"I told you, Tim. His genetic and neural structure is perfect for the suit. Look at his smile. He's already passed the first step and doesn't even know it. Remember how you fidgeted when we did you? Squirming in your skin like you had ants crawling all over you." Michelle playfully laughed.

"I know, I know. Freaked me the hell out. Felt like my skin was on fire and each wisp of air just fanned the flame. Not good, but once I got the Suit on it felt so much better." Tim replied with the look of a memory best forgotten.

"Come over towards me, Todd and let's get you fitted. Your skin is so fresh right now. So sexy, like a petite nana. I would like to touch it everywhere. It is so soft and supple, like a newborn. Not a single hair." she said with a very amused expression.

Catching my reflection in the glass I noticed I was bald from head to toe. No one had mentioned that. Not a hair anywhere, eyebrows included. Thank God I still had eyelashes, or I would look like a complete freak. "What happened to all my hair?"

"Oops dog, left that detail out, didn't I? Didn't want you to go postal so I let it slide. My bad!" Tim laughed his way through his answer. "No worries, stud. It will all grow back in a few weeks, and you will be your new studly self."

"I like him without the hair, so smooth. It makes him look like a newborn. I think it's cool!" piped in Michelle.

Walking toward Michelle I could see a glass closet where a shimmering silver piece of material seemed to float in midair. "Is that my suit, Michelle?" I asked nervously. It was weird looking.

"Yes. Each Suit is unique to the individual. You cannot use Cat's, or mine or Tim's. After the Suit has assimilated your information and bonded with your neural pathways it is only for you. Mon cher, to attempt to use another's, would short-circuit your nervous system. It won't kill you, but it would be very unpleasant." she said with a serious look. "With that said, let's get started. Ready, Tim?"

With a seriously grave look he replied, "Yes. Activate assimilation procedure x -14dz. Subject Todd Peters. Introduction protocol complete. Viral and bacterial scan complete. Cold laser defoliation complete. Subject ready for neural implantation."

This did little to quiet a growing knot in my stomach.

"Todd, for your own well-being, do exactly what we say, when we say it. It's paramount that you follow our directions to the letter. Failure to do so can and will result in grievous harm to you. You ready?" Tim instructed.

I felt a sharp stab of fear. I hoped they couldn't see or sense how nervous I was. This seemingly happy-go-lucky guy was suddenly talking to me like I was in mortal peril. The seriousness in his voice was no joke. There was more to this man than I had expected. Lesson learned, I thought.

"Affirmative."

"Michelle, we ready? Cat, we ready?"

Michelle responded with a nod of her head, and I heard

Catherine's affirmative response. She sounded concerned and it did little to quiet my fears as she continued.

"Todd, the first few moments when the Suit comes in contact with your skin are critical, so attempt to stay as still as possible. The Suit will introduce fibrous nerve tendrils into your skin bonding with the nerve endings of every muscle and your cerebral cortex. After it has successfully bonded, Nimmrod will run a diagnostic test to make sure it has bonded with all your nerve centers. Now, this is important. Do not, and I repeat, do not under any circumstance touch the suit as it envelopes your body. The sensation will not be pleasant. It will feel like a million tiny needles pricking your skin everywhere. It will last approximately forty-five seconds but is a little different for everyone. This is a one-time experience, as the Suit will leave the neural tendrils just below the skin. When you don it, from here forward it will be like slipping on a pair of pajamas. If you reach or attempt to touch yourself when the Suit activates, you will cause a short circuit in that area, as it will get many more tendrils than it needs. And trust me when I say that is a very bad thing. It would basically render that part of your anatomy useless and dead as the overload of neural excitation would explode all the existing nerve endings. Are we clear?" Catherine spoke with a tone of gravity in her voice that I had not heard from her to this point. I could just make her out behind a glass window. She looked like she was wearing a doctor's frock.

The sudden desire to run was compelling. I was trusting my life to complete strangers. What if I'm just a guinea pig for some extreme experiment, I thought. Then, amid the panic, I suddenly experienced a calm I had never felt before. For the first time in my life, I was going to do something on faith. It was hard to explain, but I trusted these people like I had known them all my life. For once, a leap of faith was in order, and I was ready for this journey to begin.

"Yeah, go ahead when you are ready. Let's get this over with."

The Suit moved towards me like it was floating on air. As far as I could tell, it was supported by nothing. I stood perfectly still as it approached, and my mind slipped into the trance-like state we call mook yung in martial arts, or silent thinking. I felt calm and relaxed and ready for what was next. I was wrong; very, very wrong. As the Suit enveloped my body the urge to tear it off was overwhelming. It burned like I was on fire; it stung like a thousand bee stings, and I felt as if a million hypodermic needles were piercing every square inch of my skin. It covered me from head to toe and everywhere in between. The only things left uncovered were my eyes, nose and mouth. A loud groan escaped my lips, as the pain was almost unbearable. I resisted the temptation to fall to my knees, remembering Cat's warning about not letting any part of my body touch another. It was too much, and I felt myself start to lose consciousness. As suddenly as it began, it was over. The rush of endorphins was extraordinary. Every bad sensation was replaced with a calming warmth. It felt fantastic. In a few short moments I felt better than I ever had.

"Assimilation of Todd Peters complete. Nimmrod is running the diagnostic. Stay still for just a few seconds more." Catherine instructed.

Michelle looked at me with a small tear in the corner of her brilliant green eyes. "It hurts a little bit, no?"

"No, Michelle, it hurt a lot."

"Dude, that was intense, we thought you might pass out for a second. Freakin' stings just a bit, eh?" Tim said.

"Todd. Come over to the bed on the far side of the room. There, you will spend the first night as Nimmrod performs its baseline measurements and begins the basic programming sequences. The very worst is over. There was no way to prepare you for that experience. We all feel for you, as each of us has gone through the same thing." remarked Catherine as she motioned me towards her. She had a relieved expression on her face. That helped me relax more. If she was happy with my results so was I.

As I approached the bed I marveled at my mind. To be in that much pain a few short seconds ago, and then feel such a state of bliss. What an amazing organism we live in and so often take for granted. The mind's ability to forget pain is amazing, but I suppose it is like a safety net. If we experience something that the body thinks will harm us it sends signals asking us to stop. When the Navy Seals train, they find a way to get their minds to ignore the signals and push through the pain. I wondered if Nimmrod would help me do the same.

The bed looked like nothing out of the ordinary. I was so wrong. I reminded myself that things here are not as they seem. Catherine motioned me forward and I was surprised at how agile I felt. It was like the Suit was an extension and enhancer of all my body's movements.

"Lie down, Todd, and I will hook you into Nimmrod. The bed will monitor all your body functions and keep you at your preferred comfort level. This bed will be moved to your room after tonight and is now yours. A similar bed is in each of the retreats, and we will send programming to everyone. The bed will establish a baseline of your comfort needs, but you can also instruct it. Just speak plainly about what you desire, and it will respond. Too firm, too soft, too warm too cold, harder pillow, softer pillow, all these commands can be spoken, and the beds' mechanisms will comply." she said with a look of pride.

She looked kind of cute in the smock. I wonder....

As I climbed into the bed and laid down, it immediately began to adjust to my body shape, like a Tempurpedic on steroids.

"How does it feel? Is it comfortable, and do you have all that you need? When I activate Nimmrod it will send you into a deep rem sleep and begin its programming. Nothing special tonight, just some baseline information, and Nimmrod will integrate with you and the Suit."

"It feels great, and I think I'm fine." was my sleepy reply.

"You already have done a great job. she said tenderly. "Until tomorrow. Rest easy. We will see you in the morning."

As I awoke my mind was racing. What had just happened? Slowly I became aware of my surroundings and started to remember fragments of my dreams. If they were dreams. What a night. As my awareness increased, I began to sense a feeling of vitality and intellect I had never experienced before. The sensation was odd but exhilarating at the same time. I felt a physical prowess that I couldn't wait to try out. My mind was moving at a million miles an hour trying to make sense of all the random information that was streaming into it. As I sat up, I saw Catherine approaching.

"Well, good morning, you sexy man. Did you sleep well? Hold still for a moment and we will disconnect Nimmrod, and then you can rise. From here forward the bed will attach and detach from the device when you are wearing the Suit."

She was dressed in a combat jump suit with her hair in a ponytail. No makeup and looking well rested. I marveled at her beauty.

"Oui, mademoiselle, très excellent." I realized that I could speak French. I thought I could speak Spanish and German as well, although I'd never studied any of those languages at all.

"I see some of the overnight programming has taken effect. I caution you to move and think slowly for a few hours and allow your mind and body to assimilate the changes to your neural pathways."

"Okay. Can I stand up yet?"

"Of course, but don't be surprised if you are a little wobbly for a moment or two."

"How do I remove the Suit? There doesn't seem to be any buttons or a zipper of any kind."

"Do you remember yesterday when you first saw the Suit? It seemed to be suspended in midair with no visible means of support. It was a holographic projection infused with subatomic nano-bots. So, when the suit glided to you, it was a projection of your body shape with nano-bots riding on the laser streams. As soon as it approached you, your electrical field or Aura if you prefer, energized the Suit. It became a solid, attaching the neural tendrils to your nervous system. To remove it we will just reverse the procedure. The Suit now knows the frequency of your electrical field. So, to remove it, take this device and press the button marked "disengage." This will change the polarity long enough for the Suit to disengage from your body and float back to its case. We are working on a portable model for travel, but so far, we need a docking station to hold the Suit in stasis."

I looked at Catherine with a stunned look on my face. This was like something directly out of Roswell. I could hardly believe what I was hearing. The device was small, no bigger than a micro cell phone with only two buttons. "Engage" was red and "disengage" was green. It was simple. I couldn't begin to understand the technology.

"Catherine, this device could make the human race a society of geniuses."

"You are right, Todd. But knowledge without wisdom can be a dangerous thing. I don't think mainstream society is ready for this yet. So, tell me, how do you feel?" She gazed at me intently.

"I feel light, like I could walk on air. My body feels supple and more athletic than anything I've ever experienced. My mind is running at a million miles per hour with all sorts of random thoughts. Some clever; some just seems like mumbo jumbo."

"Well, it sounds like Nimmrod is doing its job. The musculature sensitivity is from the device reshaping your neural pathways. Your body will move with more economy of motion and a fluidity that only world class athletes possess."

"You know, I think you are right, I can see how this technology in the wrong hands could very easily create an imbalance in the playing field."

"As far for your brain, it will quiet down in an hour or so as all the new information is compartmentalized. Soon you will be able to pull up information as you need it. This training will continue for the next thirty days. At the end of that time, you will possess the athletic responses and enough languages and information to be effective in any country anywhere."

"I feel like I could converse on any topic at any level. And all that after only a few hours of sleep!" I marveled.

"Todd, you have been out for three days. The first segment of programming takes up to 96 hours. You were able to assimilate everything in just 72 hours. So, a 'well done' in is order. Take off the Suit, get dressed and come downstairs for some breakfast. You must be hungry by now." She looked at me with an amused smile on her face.

As I removed the suit, it felt and looked weird as it floated across the room. Like a cartoon where a ghost just floats off. I thought to myself how good I felt.

The next few months were a blur. Meals, training, Suit, sleep. After thirty days, I stopped wearing the Suit while sleeping, and only put it on occasionally for specialized instruction. So much information and so many skills were introduced to me. All the team was incredible, each a master in their own discipline. I occasionally made love to Catherine. It was always extraordinary, and I wished for more.

The driving and weapons portions were all Tim. His expertise blew me away. My stock of him went through the roof, and I hoped he would always be around when I needed him. We went to a track they had rented and did defensive driving maneuvers. Skid and recovery skills. And we used a vehicle that could do a complete rollover. I was not a big fan of that. The weapons training was much more thorough than in my Army days. Stationary firing, urban assault training, sniper training, and my favorite, hostage recovery.

Michelle's combat edge training was enlightening. I had never thought of using a playing card as a weapon. She was a master, showing me that anything within reach had the potential to become a self-defense tool. Her knowledge of martial arts was expansive, and I honed new skills. It was fun, as she could be silly and playful. I wanted to make love to her again, but our days were filled with training. It seemed like years since we'd had our moment. We also spent time on etiquette and how to interact abroad. The basic information was there from Nimmrod, but she managed to fill in the nuances.

Catherine was gone quite a bit, doing whatever she does Managing resources and doing intel on the next project was my guess. She was closed mouthed about what was next.

When she was around, there was a deep sense of urgency. I got the impression that the training was about to end, and we were ready to take on the next project. I was right. Almost six months to the day, she called us into her private office. I had not seen her office. It was furnished with antique furniture, plush rugs, and exquisite pieces of art. She was dressed in a red business suit with her hair done in a French braid.

"Okay, team, it's crunch time. William Potts, our latest client, is on the verge of completing a device that potentially could change the military landscape forever. He is quite brilliant. He was educated at Oxford and graduated with his doctorate from MIT at the ripe age of twenty-three. It seems he is starting to attract the attention of more than one group who would like to take advantage of him and his discoveries. I know most of the players who are looking at him and suffice it to say they are not what I consider friendlies. We need to intercede in order to protect him and his device. There will be an operational meeting at seven tomorrow morning. Get some rest and I will see you then. Everyone, wear your Suit tonight, and Nimmrod will infuse into your minds all the intel we have at this moment."

Chapter 4 – The Mark

Catherine looked a little anxious. Apparently, the clock was ticking. “We don’t have much time. William is very close to realizing a working prototype of his invention. We need to get to him in the next twenty-four hours. Todd, you and Tim will run point and Michelle and I will be rear guard and relocation. Nimmrod has provided you with the location and basic intel. Michelle has made all the travel arrangements. Tim has assembled the necessary gear to make this a success and Todd is ready with the extraction route and transportation needed to move William and his equipment to a new lab. Both jets are on this coast and flight plans have been filed. Load the Hummer and get the gear to the jet. Good luck, and are there any questions?”

Tim responded first. “Yes, did our associates get the vehicles we asked for delivered to the strip, and are the personnel at the hangar?” He looked all business in black military fatigues.

“They did, and I have satellite confirmation that they are in Hangar B waiting for us to arrive.” Michelle responded.

“Does William have any idea that we are coming?” I asked.

“Yes, I’ve been in touch with him for the past year and we have become good friends. He knows our efforts to protect and serve the greater good. He realizes that we are not here for monetary gain or fortune. Our goal is to protect budding inventors and their inventions. To help them develop their property safely and get it to market how they want to, or not, if they so desire. Our nemesis, Dark Matters, is snooping around electronically, so be prepared for anything. We don’t think they have Williams’ physical location, but with their resources, it’s only a matter of time.” Catherine replied.

As we made our way to the elevator and then the garage, I felt a nervous excitement in the pit of my stomach. It was the fluttery feeling of going on a first date. Or when you’re getting ready to take the field in a football game. Different for everyone I guess, but I have never gotten used to it.

“Relax, Todd and trust the training. It’s like a football game, after the first hit, it’s all instinct. You are going to do great. I’ve never had such a talented student as you. You were so easy to train, and your grasp of multiple disciplines and techniques is amazing. So chill, bro, and let's go make some history." Tim extended his hand for a fist bump. And with that we were on our way.

William looked like an English version of Albert Einstein. He had crazy hair and small horned rimmed glasses perched on a decidedly English nose. He was a tall slender man, six foot four or so, maybe 185 pounds soaking wet, with piercing green eyes and an easy charismatic smile. His athletic build suggested that he had played Lacrosse or soccer. He opened the door as soon as I rang the bell.

"Mr. Potts, I'm Todd Peters. I believe you are expecting us. By the way, Lancaster rules." I said with a calm expression, using the code that Catherine had given me.

"Yes, that's correct, my old soccer team. Come in and let's get started." William anxiously replied.

"Tim will pull the truck up to the service door and we'll get loaded." I signaled Tim that Potts was ready.

"Oh, thank you. Something doesn't feel right. I've had the feeling that I am being watched. And strangers have been asking questions of my friends and neighbors." was his nervous reply.

We quickly loaded all of William's gear. It only took about half an hour, and we were ready to go. William and I jumped into the van, while Tim drove. "Okay, let's get out of here." I said.

"That could be trouble." Tim pointed at two black SUVs that flew past us. He spoke into his wrist mike. "We have a development. I believe DM is on the way to William's place. I don't think they recognized us, but it won't be long before they figure it out. I am moving to alternate route C. Please inform the other vehicle. Over."

"Affirmative, decoy has already been deployed, and we will see you at the hangar. Last transmission." Catherine replied tersely.

The rest of the twenty-minute ride was uneventful, but I had the sensation we had just dodged a bullet. We pulled into the hangar and closed the doors. I noticed several people outside armed and on patrol. As we got out of the vehicle everyone breathed a sigh of relief. It was short lived. Catherine began barking orders like a military general.

"All right, everyone, move. We have ten minutes to get loaded and in the air. We miss that window, and all hell will break loose. DM acquired satellite imagery of our truck and will be here shortly. The decoy bought us maybe fifteen minutes, but believe me, they are on the way."

Six men came out of the shadows and began transferring the equipment to the two jets. We were loaded in about five minutes and boarding the plane. William nodded in our direction as he entered the plane with Michelle and Catherine. "Later, gents. Thank you."

Tim and I boarded the other jet, the hanger doors opened, and we began to taxi out to the runway. As we lifted off to the safety of the sky, Tim pulled up the local satellite images for the area. With a resolution of less than a meter, we saw two SUVs headed to the airport in a big hurry. If they were Dark Matters, they had just missed us. I had an uneasy feeling we would hear more from them soon, but for now, I could rest easy with the knowledge that my first mission had gone well.

A satellite call came through on the screen and Tim answered. It was Catherine. She sounded a lot more at ease, thankfully. I could make out William and Michelle in the background talking earnestly.

“How is it going over there?” Catherine asked.

“Pretty good.” I replied. “If I could just get this rush to quiet down, I would be better.”

“I know what you mean, as I never get quite used to the excitement of the moment. We cut that one close. I knew William was of interest to DM but did not think they were that close. We will land at Heathrow Airport and taxi to a private hangar. I don’t think DM has this jet’s signature or call letters, but we will take no chances. When we arrive at the hangar there will be a small team waiting to transfer William’s gear to a waiting truck. Michelle and I will be in one of the Range Rovers while you and Tim will take the other. They will proceed to the warehouse whose location is programmed into the GPS. There the equipment will be loaded into another truck. Todd, you will drive the new truck while Tim will take rear guard. The team we employ from this area can be trusted, but if they don’t know where the final location is then that information can't be extracted from them if they were to fall into the wrong hands. The coordinates to the new location are in the handheld GPS in the gear bag. In the truck and both Range Rovers there are signal scramblers that will prevent either phone or accurate GPS signals from being detected. So far, it is looking good, and I believe we can get to the new lab without incident. This retreat is in the country and very secluded. The house is off the grid, and we haven't used it for several years. It's always good to rotate assets. The technology, as far as threat detection goes, is military grade or better. It is a small fortress. The armament on the grounds could stop a small army either from the land or air. We have our own power supply in a deep bunker and short of an all-out assault we will be fine. Everyone has their instructions. Have a good flight and see you on the ground. Cat out."

I thought to myself, wow she is in charge. Her attention to detail and level of preparedness is extraordinary. She runs the show like a military op. Clean and smooth with great attention to detail. She always seems to be one or two steps ahead of my thinking, and hopefully everyone else's.

"Pretty badass, isn't she? And you just thought she was good in the sack. She's amazing, and of all the things and people and places I've been in my career, she is the most prepared of any of them. I don't know how she does it, but I'm down with her doing it. I don't have the patience or the mind to coordinate all the details." said Tim.

"Aw bull don't sell yourself short. It seems everyone on this team is capable."

"I guess I should've said I don't want to screw with it. I'm a hammer and just want to nail the hell out of stuff. It's what I do best."

"I see that and hope you never have to hammer me." I chuckled.

"No worries stud, we're a team." smirked Tim.

As we began our descent to Heathrow, I reflected on that first night in the bar back in Philly. In my wildest dreams I never thought for a second, I would be here, doing this. I wondered for a moment if my parents would have been proud. I thought they would, as I was engaged in something that could affect the shape of mankind's future.

The rest of the night was uneventful. As Catherine promised, we pulled into a private hangar at Heathrow, cleared customs and began to offload the planes. Getting into our assigned vehicles, we headed out toward the northern coast of England. It was a full moon, and the glow of the English countryside made everything look bright and surreal. After a couple of hours, we pulled up into a gated entrance to what looked like an orchard. All the trees were in neat rows. The house was invisible from the road. As we drove up the winding gravel drive, out of the corner of my eye I detected a laser sweeping the area.

We pulled up onto a concrete slab. Once we had stopped, the slab began a slow descent into the ground. Just as in Philly, I knew it was headed for the underground garage. One by one, we followed suit until all three vehicles were in the safety of the garage.

As we exited the vehicles, I could see Catherine already giving orders. Two men were beginning to offload William's equipment onto dollies as a rather robust woman made her way to Catherine. She was a large, light complected woman with bright red hair, and hazel eyes, dressed in a floral shift with a scarf around her neck. Her hair was shoulder length and a little on the tousled side. She looked Irish, or Welsh. She wrapped Catherine in a warm embrace.

"Todd, come over here please and meet not only a dear friend, but my mentor."

"So, this is the lad you've been playing up to me. A bit on the scrawny side for a yank—I thought he would be bigger." The stranger winked at me.

"I, er, well, I . . ." I stammered.

"Oh my, hasn't he met Nimmrod yet? Seems his vocabulary would be a bit on the cheeky side if he had."

"No, I can speak, just suffering a bit from sleep deprivation and jet lag. I'm Todd."

"I know who you are, lad. Give us hug; I'm just shakin' the dog on you." she laughed as she squeezed the pudding out of me. "My name is Rachel, but you can call me Mum."

Just then Tim and Michelle came over and gave Mum hugs as they all grinned. "Aw, my sweeties, how is everyone? It's been too long since we've seen each other. Let's all go up to the kitchen and get some food."

We walked through the garage, and I noticed how similar the layout was to Philly, although the vehicles were different. We walked to a blank wall, and as in Philly, were granted access after being scanned. "Good morning, Catherine. What floor would you like to access?" Elle greeted us.

"Main floor, please." Catherine replied.

The elevator opened into the kitchen area, which had a big open fireplace at one end, and a large rectangular table about ten feet from the fireplace. We all grabbed a plate and walked around the kitchen island, filling them buffet style. There was a smorgasbord of English and American food. Meatloaf, potatoes, Shepherd's Pie, burgers, fries, as well as breakfast dishes. It wasn't long before we were all sitting down at the table and digging in. Suddenly I was famished and couldn't remember the last time we had eaten.

"What time is it?" I asked.

"About midnight, Philly time, five a.m. local. We've all been up for a while." replied Catherine.

The two men from downstairs joined us and Mum introduced them. “The burly one on the end is Thumper and his evil twin is Josh. No direct blood tie, but they act and move as identical twins. ‘Tis uncanny how they seem to know each other’s every move before it happens. They are my babies, and I love them. Box them about when they screw up, right, boys?”

In unison they replied “Yes, Mum.”

The next hour was a blur. Everyone ate and laughed and caught up. William and I were the obvious strangers, but we both felt welcome.

“There will be a meeting at two in the solarium meeting room. You should be able to get a few hours’ sleep at least. It will be a busy day. Mum, will you show Todd to his room?” Catherine asked.

“You got it, love, and sweet dreams, at least for today. Things will get a bit on the rowdy side the next few weeks. Kisses.” Mum said as she began to take us to our rooms. Thumper and Josh stayed behind on KP.

By the time I got to my room, got undressed and hit the sheets, I was out in about ten seconds. The bed was perfect, just like the one in Philly.

How cool is that? I mused as I drifted off to sleep.

Chapter 5 – The Device

"What the hell!" I woke with a start and for a moment I didn't know where I was. My bed had sent a mild shock through me as a wake-up call. It was not unpleasant, but definitely woke my butt up.

I popped out of bed and did my usual stretches. I had a great sense of impending adventure. We had only heard bits and pieces about William's invention. This afternoon he would tell us what it was all about, and I could hardly wait. I bounded down the back stairs into the kitchen and grabbed a plate. Mum again had a buffet laid out, and several members of the team were chowing down. Thumper, Josh and Tim were about halfway through brunch. Everyone was dressed in regular clothes today, jeans, t-shirts, and sweatpants. Except Mum, she had on a shift dress and her ever present apron. As I rounded the island and headed for the table, Catherine and Michelle arrived. They were both in yoga attire, like they had just finished a workout.

"Good morning, everyone." Catherine said with a light-hearted air.

"Good morning." the chorus came from those of us seated.

"Did everyone get enough sleep? How does everyone feel about the new wake up alarm?" she asked.

"Caught me by surprise, Cat." was my reply.

"Let me ask you, Todd. When you awoke did you feel wide awake and ready for anything?"

"Now that I think of it, I did. I could've easily responded to a situation."

"That was my intention. In lieu of someone standing watch, the retreat's security system is tied to Nimmrod which is tied to you and your sleeping areas. If we need to wake or there is a threat detected Nimmrod will warn and wake all of us simultaneously, while arming the retreat's defenses. It's an interesting bit of software, if I do say so myself. You can thank William -- or not -- personally for that." Catherine smiled.

"Well, a little heads up would have been nice. Freaked me the hell out." said Tim looking slightly peeved.

"I was lookin' for a bloke's head to pop." said Thumper as he wielded a fork of food to his mouth. He was a big man. Polish origin or maybe Ukraine. I guessed he weighed around 300 pounds and looked as solid as a defensive tackle for the Green Bay Packers. Not a lot of fat that I could see. He ate his food with a look of pure pleasure. "Shockin' me grapes awake like that. Ain't right, a man's got feelins'." but he had a smirk on his face.

"I kinda like it. Felt good to me, and I just lay there enjoying the sensation. It didn't quit till I got out of bed. Nice." Josh grinned.

"I think it scrambled your eggs, mutton head." Thumper replied, shaking his head.

"I'm sure everyone will adapt. We will introduce it to all the retreats." Catherine explained. "All right, let's finish up and head to the solarium on the fifth floor. See everyone there in ten minutes, and William can dazzle us with his brilliant intellect."

As we entered the solarium, my mouth dropped in appreciation for what we saw.

"Puttin' on the dog a bit, hey?" said Mum with a wry smile.

I was speechless. The table was probably twenty feet long and could easily seat twenty people. It was a plank table and appeared to be solid oak. It had a hand rubbed finish with the oak's natural grain showing through. It was breathtaking. The seats were high backed and hand carved oak, and the detail was superb.

"It's beautiful." I offered.

"Believe it or not, it came from a castle in Nottingham and is approximately 580 years old. Have you noticed the solarium glass yet?" Catherine said with admiration.

I looked up to see the domed ceiling. It was inspirational, filled with stained leaded glass. Beautiful country scenes adorned the panels, each told a story. The whole home was old country, and it was obvious that the artisans who put this together left a part of their soul in each cut of wood, stone, and glass.

"This retreat was originally a lord's home. When we acquired it, we updated all the systems but left the architecture as original as we could, given the requirements we had for security." Catherine explained with a hint of pride in her voice.

We sat and got comfortable as William entered the room. He wore pleated trousers with a white shirt and plaid vest. A blue bow tie rounded out the look. Tousled hair and all, he looked inventive.

"Josh, would you drop the screen and black out the ceiling so that we can get started?" asked Catherine.

"Certainly, milady, at your service." Josh's laughingly replied.

With that William took center stage. "Okay everyone, without further ado, let me show you what I have been working on for the last six years of my life. I will explain it in layman's terms as best I can. Please hold your questions until I have finished my presentation." he said with a theatrical flourish.

"By all means begin." said Catherine. "We have a lot to do today, and some of the team will be leaving shortly."

"I know Nimmrod has supplied you with my basic biography and other pertinent information. When I was at MIT, I met a fellow student, Yong Pak. We both had a passion for nano tech and pursued it with every waking moment. We were inseparable and found a synergy between us that was unimaginable. For each problem I posed he had an answer. When he became stumped, I filled in the blanks. When I was ready to quit, he pulled me off the ledge and we marched forward. What we found in all our research was that all things have a unique frequency, a vibratory level. Water, air, solids, even flesh all have a different frequency, but share some baseline properties. And that, my dear friends, is where the excitement began. We believed that if you could identify the frequency of an object at the subatomic level you could manipulate the existing atomic structure. In other words, we believed we could take a piece of paper, introduce the proper vibratory excitation, and make it as transparent as air, so that anything might pass through it. Or make it as hard as cold rolled steel or carbon fiber and virtually impenetrable. We were on the verge of a discovery that would change everything. Any natural resource or material, organic or synthetic, could now be capable of becoming anything else. Water to food, sand to housing, suddenly all things could become all things. It seemed to be a science fiction replicator of sorts, but capable of so much more."

We sat on the edge of our seats listening intently to this man. William couldn't wait to share every detail with us.

"Our problem arose when our equipment was not sensitive enough, and did not possess the necessary power, to effect lasting change at the subatomic level. We could manipulate some elements and frequencies easily, but they lost their properties as soon as the power was removed. Sensitivity from a frequency perspective and enough power to hold the change until the atoms accepted the revision were our baseline problems. We saw no danger or possible ill effects of our experiments. Unfortunately, we were wrong." he said sadly.

"We discovered that close exposure to the item being restructured caused small anomalies in the human cellular structure. The frequency bleed was not good for humans. Now our problem, along with everything else, became containment. We were thinking of a global change and suddenly our hard work and years of trial and error had been reduced to basically test-tube examples of our invention. Yong was beside himself with anger—to him, we had failed. However, I saw it as just another challenge. In a rage, he quit, and I could not persuade him otherwise." William shook his head. "The last I heard he had been hired by another group to continue his work. It was a shame; we were a great team. I was devastated, lashed out at everyone and became reclusive. And then, I met Catherine. She encouraged me and funded me, asking nothing in return but my silence until I had perfected the device. She is truly a remarkable woman, and I have the deepest respect for her and her view of the world. Thank you, my dear Catherine!" He looked at Catherine, and you could see the deep appreciation in his eyes.

"William, you dear man, it is and always will be my pleasure to watch you grow and become the amazing human being your destiny has prepared you for." Catherine said with a humble, soft loving tone.

"So, there I was: containment, frequency degradation and low power supply. These things loomed large and could not be fixed easily in my last location without arousing suspicion. We have prepared a lab here and put all the power requirements in place. I need a few key pieces, and with those in hand I believe I can have the device operational in a couple of months." William said with a profound sense of certainty.

We all began to talk at once and attempted to yell questions over each other.

"Bloody hell, not all at once." Mum boomed. "You all will get a chance to ask your questions. William, are you ready?"

"Almost, one last thing, from a safety perspective. Until I have the containment issue figured out, I believe everyone who comes to the lab should wear their Suit. It seems to provide a margin of protection from cellular frequency decay." William admonished.

"We will advise Nimmrod and make it a safety protocol." Catherine stated." Michelle, why don't you go first."

"Oui, Mademoiselle. William, my question to you is, if you alter the frequency of an item does it displace the energy of another item?"

"No, I have found that not to be a problem as all we are doing is altering the vibratory level at the subatomic level and using existing atoms to alter the physical characteristics of the original object. No alarming side effects from that perspective."

"Thumper, you're next." Catherine directed.

"Well then, bloke, can I make my hand into a weapon like a MAC-10 or a Glock machine pistol?" he asked with a grin.

Amused by his question, William responded, "Not really, not yet. What I can do is change the vibratory level of existing cells or atoms. I will be able to make your arm as hard as steel or as transparent as air, once I get the human cell anomaly problem solved."

"Todd, you have a question?" said Catherine.

"Professor, can you make a skintight suit that I can wear under my clothing and charge it in such a way as to be impervious to gunfire or bladed attacks?" I thought it seemed like a good way to introduce everyday body armor.

"Great question again. This is a smart bunch. That is the project Catherine has me most focused on for a first application, a bulletproof pair of long johns. Supple and breathable, yet virtually impenetrable. The trick is to get the garment to dissipate the energy transfer from the projectile. Otherwise, even though it might not penetrate the suit, the force of impact could be just as deadly to human tissue."

"Any more questions?" asked Catherine.

"Aww, love could ye shave a few kilos off me portly frame?" giggled Mum.

"I'll work on it." was William's reply amidst the quiet laughter of the team. "Well, if there are no more questions right now, I'll get back to the lab, and leave you to what you do, whatever that is." he said with a chuckle as he left the room.

Catherine stood up. "Okay, then let's get to it. Michelle and Todd, you are headed to Croatia to secure the last piece of equipment to make William's device work. William calls it NAT or Nanosizer Autotransformer. It is basically a Nano transformer that reduces current down to a level that we can use. The one you will retrieve takes the current down to thirty nanohertz or 1mum squared. William will then further refine it to the level which will work for us. You will fly into Dubrovnik and follow the instructions in the packet on board the plane. One of the yachts will be in port and available for use. Use the detection and evade protocol that Nimmrod implanted. And above all trust your gut. If it feels wrong, it usually is. There are two exit strategies depending on complications or detection. You leave within the hour. Your passports and everything you need are in the wardrobe. Thumper will drive you to the plane. Now come here that I might kiss those sweet lips."

This brought an amused chuckle from the group as no one was sure if she meant me or Michelle.

Chapter 6- Detection

The next hour was a blur as Michelle and I found ourselves in the wardrobe picking out clothing, reviewing our passports and packing for a two-to-three-day trip. We were to be a newlywed couple on honeymoon in the Adriatic. My anticipation was through the roof.

Michelle grabbed me by the arm and whispered in my ear. "Mon ami, slow and easy, breathe, relax and let your training guide you. I hope we have time for some newlywed fun, non?"

Just her hand on my arm calmed me, and for a moment I realized just how much of a rookie I was. I wondered why Catherine had not sent Tim or Josh since they were much more qualified. Perhaps it was my excitement that made it appear more natural than two seasoned pros.

Before we knew it, we had said our goodbyes and were in a Range Rover headed to a private airstrip just a few miles away. As we pulled up to the plane, I took a deep breath. I can do this, I told myself. Trust the training.

We boarded the jet, the door closed, and in a few moments, we were airborne. As we reviewed the briefs left for us onboard, it became apparent that this was no ordinary piece of equipment. It was actively being sought by several groups, and the pressure to secure and transport it to our location suddenly became real.

"Michelle, why did Cat choose me instead of Tim or Josh?" I asked.

"Do you not know? You are a new face and have never been profiled. I have not been on a lot of missions either, so we are as obscure a couple as Cat could come up with in the short time frame. We will be fine, and the more natural we act the better. So, kissing, hugging, holding hands, looking at me adoringly are to be expected and will go a long way to protect our cover, oui?"

"That's what I thought. Believe me, it won't be hard to act like I'm in love with you."

"You are fun. We will be just fine."

Again, I had that feeling of being out of my element. Tim was right though, when we secured William, it was a bit dicey for a moment or two, and I had responded without thinking. Trust the training, I reminded myself and was soon able to relax and enjoy the flight.

In no time, we landed at the Dubrovnik airport and cleared customs. I felt light and confident. Michelle had a calming effect on me and made me feel very protective. Which was a joke, because I was pretty sure she could kick my butt. What made it strange for me was I think she knew it. I decided to concentrate on being her lover. We entered a private limo and headed to the hotel, and I relaxed thinking, now this is the way to travel.

The hotel was more luxurious than any hotel I had ever stayed in before. The floors were marble, and the wall coverings looked to be velvet. The trim on the ceiling was ornate and gilded.

We were in the Honeymoon Suite. The crown moldings were the same ornate trim as in the lobby. The walls were paneled in what looked like Roku, in the Teak family of woods. The sculpted carpet made the room whisper quiet. The furniture was eclectic with examples of English and Italian pieces in the room. When the porter delivered our bags, Michelle wrapped her arms around me and gave me a long luxurious kiss. I blushed noticeably and realized in an instant that was the intended reaction.

"Honey, that embarrassed me a little." I grinned at Michelle.

"Mon cher, tip this nice man so that we might enjoy our room." she coyly replied.

I tipped him, he smiled slightly, and tipped his hat. "Have a fabulous evening sir, madam, and if there is anything we can get you, please call." The porter handed me the key card as he left.

"Let's shower and have some fun before dinner. I want that dazed look when we arrive." Michelle said with a naughty grin.

"I've wanted to jump you for several months, but it's just been so crazy. Race you to the shower." I said as I peeled my clothes off.

Michelle was one of those women who no matter how many times you see her in the flesh, you are newly awestruck by her beauty. I found myself softly sighing as she removed the last bit of her clothing. Was I really being paid for this? She came to me, and we slipped under the stream of water from the multiple shower heads, slowly caressing and kissing each other. Our passion mounted with each movement, as tenderness gave way to raw passion. Soon we were locked in a lovers' embrace, riding wave after wave of exquisite pleasure, until the climatic conclusion enveloped us both. We held one another as the water continued to caress our satiated bodies. I kissed her gently on the nape of her neck. Her sweet hug and tender kiss on my chest were all the reply I needed.

As we finished our shower and dried ourselves, I couldn't help but think how emotionally attached I had become to each of the team members. I remembered Nimmrod's instruction about being able to complete the mission at the sacrifice of another team member. I wondered if I could do that. I vowed then and there to never find out, and to do everything in my power to make that a distant chance.

Dinner was great. I had lobster and scallops which were prepared perfectly. Michelle had a local fish complete with the head. That always kind of grossed me out, but she enjoyed it. A bottle of local white wine and some after dinner espresso rounded out an exquisite meal.

Michelle and I were both constantly reviewing and assessing the room, its patrons, and all the movement around us without appearing to do so. Trusting the training to the letter seemed to be working quite well.

After a sensational night's sleep, we awoke rested and ready to go. Having breakfast on the veranda overlooking the bay was surreal. Seven short months ago I was in a bar trying to get lucky. Now I was in a five-star hotel, eating breakfast with a beautiful French woman and contemplating our next move to secure and deliver NAT to William.

Opportunities are everywhere, I mused as I began to eat my breakfast. Not knowing the hotel and its surroundings was a reason for caution. Catherine had swept the area via satellite when we arrived and had detected no visible surveillance. Michelle had swept the room for listening devices and any optical devices. It was all clear. Still, we played our roles, engaging in light newlywed conversation saying nothing about the mission. Both of us were prepped and knew exactly what, when, and where we had to be to make this a success. After showering with a little light foreplay, we dressed and headed out for a day in the town.

We shopped, we laughed, we stopped and had a delicious lunch in a quaint bistro down a side alley. The architecture in Dubrovnik had a decidedly Italian influence. One thing I noticed was how clean everything was. There was no dirt or trash on the streets! All the shops were pristine and very orderly. The houses were distinctive, with chimney stacks that looked like little houses themselves, complete with stairs, doors, and windows. I love architecture and have always admired different regional interpretations of how to live. The Basilicas were extraordinary.

Although we appeared to be randomly walking and taking in the sights as any tourists might, we were checking the area for the pickup tomorrow, looking for anything or anyone out of the ordinary. I found myself trusting my gut again and attempting to remove any hint of danger from the equation. We had completed all the reconnaissance that was needed and headed back to the room for a welcome night's sleep. The morning would prove to be interesting, to say the least, and with that thought in mind we drifted off to sleep.

My sleep was fitful. I had strange and convoluted dreams, mostly about the pending mission. In one of them I seemed to be trapped in an alley. I would open a door and step through only to find myself back in the alley. That repeated until I awoke with a start, heart pounding. Some were better, like lying on the beach and just chilling.

The next morning, we packed and secured anything that might compromise us. We then proceeded to the main lobby to check out and gave the desk instructions on the disposition of our baggage. With handbags in hand, we proceeded to the pickup point.

As we sat at a small table in the bistro we had enjoyed yesterday, I was surprised by how calm and aware I was. Michelle seemed the same.

"Todd, do you want a croissant for breakfast?" she asked. Instantly, all my senses were hyper-alert. "Croissant" was our danger word for the day and meant Michelle had detected a threat.

"Yes, and a cup of espresso would be great Michelle."

She now knew I had recognized the code and was aware. I scanned the area, attempting to detect what she had seen. It came easily. From our vantage point, we could see the fountain in the square. A family of three stood by the fountain. They didn't fit. The man was thin and waspish, pacing nervously. He was dressed in a wrinkled suit and worn shoes. The woman was slightly heavy and not paying any attention to the child. She wore an expensive tailored dress. Her purse looked to be worth more than the dress. She scanned the area, looking for us, I surmised. The child didn't look like either parent. He seemed bored and had distanced himself from the man and woman, as if acting out a role. He wore shorts, a t-shirt, and old worn-out sandals.

"Michelle, I need to use the restroom. I'll be right back."

"I will see you in a minute." she nodded.

As I entered the restroom, I began my transformation. Taking off my shirt I folded it and placed it in my bag. I now had on a t- shirt and slacks. Adding a quick moustache, a van dyke and a soft beret, the transformation was complete. I walked out of the restroom and approached the counter.

"Vincent, is my order of bagels and lox ready to go?" I asked easily in Italian.

"Yes. That will be forty euros." was the clerk's coded reply as he handed me the package containing the device.

I paid the clerk and placed the order in my bag. I calmly walked by Michelle and headed up the alley away from the square. Stopping occasionally to survey my surroundings, I concluded I was not being followed. As I approached the south end of the square, I stopped and sat on a bench. Taking a small artists pad from my bag I began to sketch the fountain and its patrons. The "family" had moved closer to the alley, and the woman was lingering in the alley opening, occasionally looking up at the bistro. I resisted the temptation to look and see if Michelle was still there. I knew she was doing her part, just as I had done, and if all went well, I would see her soon. After about fifteen minutes, I placed my pad in my bag and began to walk slowly towards the harbor.

Pausing here and there to admire the architecture and the beautiful basilicas, I vowed to come back here someday and give this town the attention it deserved. But that would have to wait.

My steps were light and sauntering. I felt like a lion ready for anything. All my senses were working in hyperdrive. From the sweet salty smell of the harbor to the distant clanging of bells from a lighthouse, sights, sounds and smells were all particularly vivid. I could smell the freshly baked bread in the air. The rich aroma of strong coffee was everywhere. The sounds of business and the light chatter of their patrons was abundant. I felt like I was being watched and just couldn't shake that feeling. I wondered if that awareness was a product of Nimmrod's infusion of neural memories, or if I was just meant for this. A little of both, I chuckled to myself.

I approached the south end of the yacht basin and stepped inside a restroom area. Quickly changing yet again I removed the hat and the van dyke, leaving the moustache. Taking off my t-shirt and folding it neatly so that it wouldn't make my bag bulge, I put on a Miami Heat basketball jersey and donned a ball cap. Slipping on a pair of Oakley's completed the transformation. Walking out of the restroom, I walked straight to the yacht moored in front of me. The captain welcomed me as if he had done so a thousand times.

"Good day, sir. Would you like to freshen up?" Captain Nicholas asked.

"Thank you, yes." I replied. Nimmrod had supplied my memories with the layout, and I walked effortlessly to the master stateroom. After changing into all Egyptian cotton shirt and pants, I made my way to the bridge. The yacht, Obsession, was a hundred and fifty feet in length. Built in an explorer style, she had a high bow and high freeboard. The bridge was one deck removed from the uppermost deck and had every conceivable electronic device I had ever seen on a boat. Some I did not recognize. Capable of oceanic crossings on her own bottom, she was an explorer class yacht in every sense of the word. From her furnishings to her equipment no expense had been spared.

After making my way from the bridge down to the aft deck I sat in one of the lounges facing the row of bistros on shore. As one of the crew, a lovely Filipino, brought me a beverage I thought to myself, I could get used to this. “Thank you, Meline.” I said automatically.

“You are quite welcome, sir. Will there be anything else?” she replied in perfect English.

“Not at the moment.” I realized I knew who the girl was, her background, and felt a familiarity that could only have come from Nimmrod.

Surveying the dockside area, I noticed a portly woman approaching the yacht. As she approached, the captain took her bags, shook her hand and welcomed her on board. Michelle? No way. This woman weighed at least 180 pounds and looked nothing like Michelle.

In a moment, we cast off for Venice. The first mate barked orders and two deck hands retrieved our dock lines. We were under power and headed out to sea. Scanning the dock, I did not see the “family. But on the south end of the dock, I saw a small flash as if a mirror or a lens had caught the light for a moment. I wondered if that was an accidental optic, or someone had just scoped us.

As Michelle joined me on the aft deck, I couldn’t help but chuckle. “That was you boarding the ship?”

"Well, of course! My disguise was good, no?" she smiled.

"It was great. I really didn't recognize you. You even walked differently with a slight limp. Just as some-one overweight might."

"I put an orthopedic in my right shoe and it gave my gait the appearance of a limp. Nimmrod is so good and makes changing into another character so easy. Don't you agree?"

"Yes. I can't remember when I have been so pumped up. I haven't felt this alive in a while."

"You are more valuable than you know." she said as she sat in a lounge chair next to me. "Cat took great care in selecting you. Out of thousands of potential can-didates, you made it to the last five and then the final selection. Your willingness to overcome your fear in the pub was the final test. She was convinced from that mo-ment forward you were the one. And just a note to you, she has never slept with a team member other than you, as far as I know, and I know her very well."

That bit of information puzzled me and sent my spirits soaring all at the same time. I suddenly felt under qualified and hoped I could live up to her expectations. One moment at a time, I reminded myself.

The rest of the evening was uneventful. Dinner was on the aft deck. Cocktails were on the bridge with the captain. The conversation was light and pleasant. We made our way to the master stateroom to catch a nap, as we were about four hours from the port of Venice. From there we planned to jet back to the retreat to deliver the last component to make William's incredible device a reality.

It seemed that we had just laid down when I awoke with a start, as did Michelle, who was spooning me in the master stateroom's bed, the shock alarm startling us. A look at the clock told me it had been several hours.

A knock came on the stateroom door. One of the stewards, Peter, opened the door. "We've been scanned. You need to get dressed immediately and prepare to disembark. Your kits have been put together, and once you've established a weapons check we'll get you on your way. Meet me and Cap on the bridge for instructions. Hurry, we think we might get boarded under the guise of a customs inspection. You both need to be off the boat before that."

We were dressed and on the bridge in less than five minutes. Michelle and I both moved with confident ease. Not hurried, but purposeful. As we entered the bridge the captain apprised us of our situation.

"About twenty minutes ago we were thermal scanned for occupants. Some of our software also detected a sat sweep of the yacht and her systems. This was followed by a sophisticated audio sweep with voice detection capabilities. We are quite sure it's DM. We believe their intent is to retrieve the device from you without regard for casualties. Consider this a Level 4 threat with combat imminent. We have placed a small Zodiac off the port side. You can enter it from the dive locker. Do a weapons check and board the Zodiac. It has a hydrogen powered outboard that gives off hardly any signature, either heat or sound. You should be able to slip away from the ship, make it to the bulkhead next to the airport, and then to Hangar 13. The flight line of the Venice airport sits along the bulkheads of this port. Peter will drop you at the correct place. Clear the fence, get to the hangar, board the plane. And good luck. We will see each other again. Now move."

We went immediately to the dive locker and did a weapons check. I loved my compact Glock machine pistol with the modified magazines that held one hundred rounds of ammo. I noticed three clips in my boogey bag and assorted flares, smoke and incendiary devices. My weapon had a silencer with flash suppressor attached. As I raised it, I noticed the balance was perfect and would not affect my sight picture at all.

"In the Zac." commanded Peter.

Michelle and I stepped in the boat, and with a soft whoosh we were off. Not a sound from the engine. The quiet displacement of water was all we heard. It was very, very stealthy.

Suddenly we saw bright flashes in the direction of the yacht. It was certainly sound suppressed automatic weapons fire. In a short twenty seconds it was over, and we could vaguely make out the silhouette of a boat slowly sinking. The yacht slipped away under power with no running lights, and suddenly I knew we were on our own. Almost immediately we detected a small craft zigzagging back and forth as if searching for something. That something was us. Peter held up a small device that detected audio and thermal sweeps.

"So far so good. The Zac has as much stealth tech as we could put on it, and I think we will make it undetected. But just in case, weapons out, locked and loaded, safety's off." Peter instructed.

"Roger." was my reply.

"Yes." said Michelle.

The next few minutes were intense. As we approached the bulkhead we noticed the small craft on an intersecting course, headed straight for us. As they came within about a hundred feet, a laser targeted our boat. Instinctively I raised my weapon and made one sweeping burst with the Glock. I felt nothing as the weapon discharged and the months of training took over in a nano second. And just as soon as it had started, it was over. Peter and Michelle sat in stunned silence.

"Todd, how in the hell did you know for sure?" asked Peter.

"Did you all not see the pinpoint laser sweep?" I replied, "My instincts told me they were a threat."

As we pulled up next to the boat my observation was correct. There were three men dead in combat dress, blacked out, sophisticated weaponry by their sides. Suddenly I felt sick to my stomach. Peter noticed and immediately drove us the final fifty yards to the bulkhead.

"Yo, Todd, first time is the worst. It is never a good thing to take a life. Unfortunately, it's the world that we live in. It's as true today as it was a hundred years ago. Exit the boat and make your way to the hangar." Peter instructed. "I'll take care of the cleanup, and we'll see you soon. If it's any consolation, thank you. That was as quick and purposeful a reaction as I've ever seen and trust me, I've seen a lot. Nicely done."

Taking my nips out of my belt, I cut the fence and we made the short dash to the hangar, walked through the door and met our pilot. The plane was prepped and ready. I was walking in a daze and glad Michelle was there to assist me. So many thoughts and emotions were running through my mind. Sure, I had shot plenty of guns. And had even thought of what it would be like to shoot at someone. But the finality of shooting and killing three men was more than I had expected. I still felt sick to my stomach and wondered how I was going to reconcile my thoughts.

In a few minutes we were safely on board and taxiing down the runway. As we lifted off, I started to come back to reality.

"Todd, let the training help. Try to relax. Nimmrod has provided neural memories to help you disassociate yourself from the act you performed in our defense." Michelle wrapped her arms around me.

"I will be okay. Just give me a few quiet moments to come to grips with the events of the last hour."

I vowed then and there never to take a life unless ours were threatened, and furthermore to do everything in my power to avoid it. The morality of the moment puzzled me. There is such a fine line between good and evil. Those men will never experience another moment on this earth, yet but for my quick actions it could easily have been us. It gave me a lot to think about. I knew I would have to come to terms with it.

As we flew into the night sky the memory of the moment softened, and I wondered to myself if that was Nimmrod or me. Unbelievably, I fell asleep. For a moment before I drifted off, I wished I were back in the Pub and viewing life from the safety of my stool.

Chapter 7 – Acquisition

Michelle gently prodded me. “We are at the airport. It’s time to get off the plane and go to the retreat.”

“Ok, babe, I am up and ready to go.” I groggily replied. The emotion of the evening had overloaded my senses. I was exhausted and needed one of Tim’s power shakes. Looking at my watch I realized it was almost six in the morning. No wonder I was so tired.

“Did you get any sleep.”

“No, Todd, I was giving Cat a sit-rep.”

As we exited the plane, the first person we saw was Tim, and in his hand were two thermoses. I could only hope they were what we thought. He handed one to Michelle and then one to me.

“Thought you two might need these after the events of last night.” he said.

“Thanks pal, I need your magic concoction this morning.” I replied.

Michelle and I both wasted no time and turned them up and began to drink as if we had just walked in from the desert.

I was a bit surprised that he had brought the armor-plated Hummer. Even though it was an H2 it was badass and could stand a direct hit from an RPG. It had run-flat tires with lightweight armor plating everywhere. Inside there was a small com center with drop down screens in front of each seat and wireless keyboards.

"Hey Tim, why did you bring the H2?"

"Been a little weird around the retreat the last two days. Nothing conclusive, just some sat sweeps and a drone flyover. We are on Alert 3 and need to get to the house. Cat needs to see you as soon as we get there, stud."

We were a bit on edge all the way to the retreat. Tim was driving fast, but not fast enough to attract any attention. Michelle was fidgety, and I had a sense of foreboding I couldn't put my finger on. The retreat looked no different than when we had left except for a glow along the perimeter.

"Tim, what is the glow all about." I queried.

"It's some weird ass shit Potts thought up. Basically, it's a plasma field that will render anything that contacts it unconscious."

Riding down into the garage, I felt a sudden sense of relief, as if I had been holding my breath. The feeling was like coming home to loved ones after a long and dangerous journey. That amused me, because that's exactly where we had been.

Catherine looked serious, and I had never seen her look so alert.

"Todd, do you have the package?" she barked.

Caught by surprise from her tone, I replied, "Yes, right here, and happy to be rid of it."

"Give it to Josh and follow me." she commanded.

For a moment I thought I was in some deep shit, but out of the corner of my eye I saw Thumper, and he gave me thumbs up. Which, coming from him, made me feel a little better.

Once in the elevator she softened noticeably and came to me. Without a word she put both arms around me and gave me the most tender hug I had ever experienced. It gave me such a sense of peace and wellbeing.

"You scared me, and I'm not used to that emotion. I didn't realize I cared for you so much. Michelle's account of the events once you boarded the yacht did little to quiet my fears. Everyone is amazed at how well you performed. Tim will debrief you and Michelle separately, and then together, which is standard protocol for a successful mission."

"I'm speechless, Cat. I had no idea you felt that way about me."

"You are the first man I have been with in a quite a while. I enjoy your company and the way you treat everyone around you. You take them at face value. No judgement. That is a big plus in my book. When Michelle sent her sit-rep I got the sudden 'what have I done?' sensation." she said as she released me from her hug and moved to the other side of the elevator.

"But from what I heard, you saved the day and responded in a manner few of us thought you would be capable of on your first outing. Peter said he had never seen anything like it. He said it was as if you had a sixth sense, knowing exactly when to fire and were as precise as a laser guided weapon, a minimum expenditure of ammunition with pinpoint accuracy. And to that I say, well done, and thank you. I'm sure you experienced what we call 'Combat Remorse.' It is not an easy thing to take a life; it's so final. It's one thing to do it from a distance, but in close quarters, it seems, and is, very real. Mum will help you with that part of your debriefing. She is very good at putting things in perspective."

All this caught me off guard. Trying to process so much was a little overwhelming. "I do feel strange about those men. I know they would have shot us without a second thought, and I think instinctively I knew that. It really was the training, and we have everyone on the team to thank. I didn't think much at all. Assess, respond and follow through, Tim must have said a million times. When the time came, I let my mind go and let the training work for the best outcome." I said somewhat confidently as I leaned up against the walls of the elevator. Man, I was ready for a shower and to get out of these clothes.

"Good evening, Todd, Catherine. What floor do you desire?" Elle asked.

"Fourth floor please." Catherine replied.

We arrived at the fourth floor and exited the elevator. We went into a private study that was lined with row after row of books from floor to ceiling. On one side of the bookcase was a floor to ceiling ladder riding on a rail. The sudden desire to get on it, give a push and ride the length of the bookcase was almost overpowering. Catherine motioned for me to sit in a beautiful red leather-bound chair. She took a position behind a desk that must have been a few hundred years old. The carving was superb and the top looked like leather.

"This desk is so precious to me. Josh built this from a three-hundred-year-old set of plans. It's exquisite."

"No kidding. I thought it was an antique. This is an amazing group of people you have assembled."

"Todd Peters, this is for you." she handed me a leather- bound portfolio.

I opened it and let out an audible gasp. Inside was a document from a bank in Zurich. My name was at the head of it and some legal descriptions followed. What caught my eye was the balance column and the end number, 3,104,700.00.

"Thank you, Todd, and may we all live long enough to enjoy the fruits of our labor. The original contract amount was three million. We had placed it in an interest-bearing account tied to our mutual fund account.

The 104,700.00 is the interest you have accrued in the last seven months. You can seek your own financial adviser, or if you like, you may join our investment group. All the team but Thumper are involved. Thumper does something a little different. You need not decide today. Instructions for accessing your funds are in the packet, and again we, the team and potentially the world, thank you for your efforts."

"Thank you." was my weak reply. I really was speechless. I had never had that much money in my entire life. That kind of money was for the elite and the very rich. To me it represented a lifetime of work, and to think I made that in seven months was mindboggling.

"We will talk more later. Right now, let's get some breakfast, debrief the both of you and let you have a conversation with Mum."

As we boarded Elle, I still was numb. I suddenly wanted to go shopping, but that was absurd as I had everything I could possibly need right here at my fingertips. When we entered the kitchen Thumper boomed, "Hey Todd, can you lend a poor bloke like me a few quid?"

"Sure Thumper." I replied to peals of laughter from everyone. There was a lighthearted air emanating from everyone. And each team member looked at me with a respect I had not seen a few short days ago. In that instant I knew this was the only family I needed, and I would protect them with every fiber of my being. As they all smiled at me in turn, I realized they also knew exactly that.

The rest of the day was as Cat suggested. We had a thorough debriefing from Tim, first alone, and then Michelle and I together. Tim's demeanor at the debriefing was very professional, and the amount of information he gathered from us surprised me. When you experience things outside of your comfort zone it's interesting how much information you retain. All you need is someone asking the right questions and it flows out of you like water.

The session with Mum, on the other hand, was not very pleasant at all. She had a Sigmund Freud mentality that exposed the underbelly of your persona. We talked for several hours about a variety of topics including the death of my parents and some other things she said I had hidden in the closet. Her job, as she put it, was to help me take all the boxes of stuff hidden in my mind's closet out into the open. Open each box in turn and look at the contents and decide whether to keep it, throw it away, or put it back into the box, and ultimately back into my mind's closet. It was a clever way to help me look inward.

"Todd, what gave you the most pause after the events of the previous night?" Mum asked.

"Well, I guess the shooting part for me was the worst." I said as I nervously fidgeted in the chair. "I had been dreading this. Up until then all the disguises and the cloak and dagger stuff was quite fun. I had never felt so alive, but then, when I shot those men, that… that was tough. My initial reaction was instinctive, but to see the result of my actions was more than I was prepared for."

"I know you have experienced all the emotions we all go through, love. Let me offer this, and we will close this session. Did you feel like you were assassinating those men or protecting Peter and Michelle? The difference is huge. Have a quick look into your brain and give me your first gut response."

"I was protecting the three of us."

"A good answer, luv. Your noggin is in good nick, and you will be fine. As long as you can differentiate between protection and assassination you will be fine. Give us hug, luv, and on your way."

And with that, it was over. Mum was the appropriate name for her. She was soft and compassionate like a mother. But there was also a firmness and resolve in her that was not to be trifled with.

The events of the last few days had exhausted me, and all I wanted to do was sleep. I checked in with Cat and Tim and went to my room. As I lay in bed watching old episodes of Gunsmoke, I knew the current path was the right one and felt at peace with all my actions and decisions. Visions of Marshall Dillon played in my head as I drifted off to sleep.

Chapter 8 – It Works

It felt like Christmas morning. At breakfast everyone talked at a million miles an hour, speculating on what Potts was about to show us. The room had that old estate feeling. With twelve- foot ceilings and heavy crown molding. A huge stone fireplace with a nice crackling fire going stood at one end. We sat at a table that could seat at least 16. We were dressed in casual clothes and helped ourselves to some of Mum's great cooking. Catherine, Tim and Mum were not at the table, and I assumed they were with Potts in the lab.

"All right, everyone, off your butts and on your feet. Down to the lab everyone and let's go see this dog and pony show." Tim barked as he entered the room.

Buzzing with anticipation, we looked like a bunch of kids on an Easter Egg Hunt as we piled into the lift and headed towards the lab. We were about to witness a demonstration of a device that could potentially change the world.

As we entered the lab, I was a bit disappointed. On a table was a laptop, and next to the table was a chair. William was standing next to a cylinder-shaped object about six feet long. Resting horizontally on a tripod it looked simple enough. It had gold rings around it every six inches or so. Five cords went into one end of it and on the other end was a small rod about three inches long sticking out. You could see frost on the tube as it sat there humming. I noticed the hair on my arms standing up and wondered if it was from the device. All of us looked at the object with a little disappointment. We had speculated it would be bigger.

"Good morning, team. said Potts eagerly.

"Good morning." we replied.

"Take a seat and we will get started. The hum you hear is the electrical current being fed into the device, which we call FEAT. This is an acronym for Frequency Enhancer and Atomic Transformer. The sensation of your hair standing on end is because of the immense electrical field being generated by FEAT. It is small, but it packs a large punch." William explained beaming with pride like he had just introduced his first child. Well, maybe he had.

As we all sat down in the chairs, I noticed Catherine was still not around. Tim and Mum were here and taking a seat. I wondered where she was.

"It has been a hectic and productive several months. Securing NAT gave us the jump start that we needed. Refined calibration was the key to the frequency degradation, and it solved the issue of the anomalies in human cell structure caused by frequency bleed. We've already discussed the device's intended capabilities. Well, I can tell you they far exceeded my expectations and Catherine's. We were not prepared for so much success so soon, and I think you will be amazed at what this thing will and can do. Super conductors are a primary component, hence our extreme power demands. Some of the memory chips that are in this are very new technology. We have been able to imprint information on the surface of a water molecule and developed a way to retrieve that information. Imagine the water molecules surface as a balloon. We are able to imprint information on its whole surface. Once we have done that the molecule stiffens and takes on a permanent solidarity until we remove all the information. This will make silicon chip technology a thing of the past. In a single glass of water there are enough molecules to store all the written information in the U.S.

"Shall we begin? An ordinary piece of paper is before you. It will rip and tear, as normal paper will. What I'm about to do is change the vibratory level of the atoms that make up the paper. First, we will speed them up to make it as transparent as air, then slow the molecules down to make it as hard as steel." he beamed.

We all looked at him like he was a mad scientist. A soft hum began to grow as Potts sat at the desk. He typed in some instructions into the laptop, and FEAT began to hum and glow a soft bluish color. At the end of the room about ten feet away was a piece of paper suspended between two towers with clamps holding it in place. I heard and saw the device but saw nothing out of the ordinary about the paper. The only thing I noticed was a distortion in the air coming from the small rod at the end of FEAT. It looked like heat haze rising from a road on a very hot day.

"Thumper, will you lend me a hand, please?" Potts asked.

"Aw right, Guvner, but I'll not lose me hand, will I?" responded Thumper with a nervous expression on his face.

"No, it's safe. I've already done it so you will be fine. Walk over to the paper and push your hand through it, please."

As instructed Thumper walked to the suspended paper and slowly pushed his hand into it. We gasped in unison. It was as if the paper were made of Jell-O. It bent and molded to his hand until finally his hand pushed through. The look on his face was priceless.

"Hey Potts, this feels a bit odd you sure it's okay?"

"You are fine, my enormous friend, and you can pull your hand out anytime."

As he did, we all looked at his hand and noticed a pinkish glow to it.

"What the hell, Potts, me mitt is pink."

"When you come into contact with the field of the device, it regenerates all the cells in the area exposed. Notice that all the scars in his hand are gone, and his skin is as soft as a newborn baby. We aren't sure if it's temporary or permanent, but with a little more investigation we should know soon. Now Thumper, touch the paper again." William directed, as he made a few keystrokes. When Thumper touched it this time, it was solid and clanked when he hit it.

"We took this same piece of paper to the range this morning and a fifty-caliber round would not penetrate it. It bounced off the paper like it was armor plating. Can you imagine armor plating that weighs the same as a piece of paper?" William glowed. "Conventional weapons would be useless, and we could create personal body armor that would stop any weaponry known to man, short of something atomic. The obvious problem is even though you can't penetrate the material you must find a way to dissipate the energy of the projectile. I'm working on that. A few things need to be ironed out, such as the power supply. It takes a good bit of power to make it all work. Once the material is energized it needs to be held in that state for at least three minutes for the rearrangement of the vibratory signature to become permanent. However, you can change it back given the same parameters. Size is also an issue. I need to figure out a way to make this portable so we can take it with us and use it to our benefit. And lastly, we need to be responsible. If this were to fall into the wrong hands, it could reshape the world overnight. Imagine an army and machines that were suddenly impervious to conventional weaponry. You could become the leader of the known world almost overnight. So, what do you all think of our invention?" Potts asked with a look like he was floating on air and had just singlehandedly shown us the greatest thing since a laptop. And to tell you the truth it was a lot more than that.

We sat stunned as the significance of his discovery sank in. With his simple demonstration he had single-handedly changed modern armor forever. My mind raced as I thought of application after application, from space exploration to scouring the ocean floors. Why, you could take the simplest material and make it as dense as a collapsing star or as transparent and flexible as the most pliable material known to man. Nothing would ever be the same. When he figures out the side effect it had on Thumper's hand and whether that was a lasting thing, did that mean immortality had just arrived?

Suddenly I was scared, and I mean, scared to my core. People would stop at nothing to get this from us and use all means at their disposal to do so. As I looked about the room, I saw the same reaction in everyone's eyes: fear and uncertainty.

William looked puzzled, as our reaction was not what he expected at all. I don't believe he comprehended the gravity of the moment.

"William, we're speechless. I think we need time to digest what we have just witnessed. We need time to let it sink in. I know I have a ton of questions I would like to ask. But maybe now isn't the right time." I said in somewhat of a state of shock.

William turned off the device, and we sat and quietly talked. The conversation was subdued and full of anxious tones. He left for his room with a wave of his hand, and I thought that perhaps he really did not understand that he had singlehandedly changed the landscape of the planet.

"Okay crew, everyone to the solarium on the top floor. We have a lot to talk about. And, like you, I'm stunned. I had no idea. We need to see what Catherine has to say. But for me that device, as cool as it is, scares the hell out of me." said Tim with as serious a tone as I had heard from him yet. I think we all felt the same way.

We collectively made our way to the solarium, unaware that just off property the group we had been avoiding was close, too close. DM was getting ready to strike.

Chapter 9 – Assault

"Son of a bitch. I said." I thought you said this location had been reconned and would be an easy entry, George."

"Sam, this tech is new to me. I was here two weeks ago and it looked like normal estate defenses." George replied.

"Augustus, is your team in place? I'm sure that Potts is here, and we are going to get him and that fucking device of his even if I have to send all three teams in." George barked.

"Piss off, mate, we are waiting on you to say the word. Let's get crackin' and roust this bitch." Augustus replied in a thick British accent.

I am tough on my team, and they respond well. My two team leaders are beyond question in loyalty and expertise. George Uri is trained by and retired from SPETSNAZ, Russia's most elite Special Forces group. He is a big robust Russian with an IQ off the charts and a desire for combat that I've not seen before—a ruthless individual with very little regard for collateral damage.

The mission is first. Fuck the rest. And if you're in the way, well then, that's your problem.

Augustus Helms, the prissy Brit. Although, to have him by your side when the shit goes down greatly increases your chances of survival, let alone completing the task. Trained by the SAS who started it all, he is perhaps the most well-rounded soldier I've ever met. And a good friend to boot. The other eight men on the team come from various backgrounds, and each has skills we sought and secured. All in all, a great collection of personnel and well equipped for the task at hand.

Me, my name is Sam Craze and I'm the leader of this collection of badasses. I am American by birth but trained abroad with most of the world's elite fighting forces. Seals, Delta Force, and my personal favorite group, those crazy bastards the Israelis' and their special little group, Shayetet 13. An intense group of men, they take training to a level that would make a SEAL whimper. Deprivation and extreme mental and physical hardships are commonplace. Their training regime goes on for months, and if you survive you indeed have been forged into a modern-day weapon.

Our objective has been to gather intel on William Potts and secure him and his device for the group we work for. We had just missed him several months ago. DM pays very well and equips us with the latest tech, so imagine our surprise when we ran up against something we had never seen.

"Augustus, you ever see anything like this? What does the infrared scanner show?"

"No reading, Sam. I don't know what it is. It looks like a plasma field of some kind. I don't think it's lethal; I don't see any dead animals around. Probably just knocks your mittens off and alerts the security system. This place is tighter than it was two weeks ago. I'm sure their whole team is inside and it's going to be a bitch. This place is in good nick. I'm sure we aren't seeing all the defenses."

Damn what a pain. We were about a click away and reconning the sight and looking for an entry. It didn't look good. I like to get in quiet and get out quick. That bitch Catherine wasn't afraid of spending big bucks on defenses. We've butted heads a few times, and she's always been just one step ahead of me.

“All right, everyone to the rally point and let’s assess what we know. Everyone be there in fifteen mikes.”

“Shit, let’s go.” said George.

“You got it, mate.” confirmed Augustus.

And with that we left our positions to regroup and discuss our options.

Tim was monitoring the security screens when the first alarm sounded. “Aw, hell no.” he exclaimed into his wrist communicator, and we all jumped to attention. “We just got a seismic alarm from about a click away. Could be anything, but we need to assume a breach. Thumper, deploy a drone for a perimeter sweep, and everyone take a station. Let’s be ready, so load William’s device and all the assorted hardware into the sub. Todd, I want you and Michelle within an arm’s length of William. Everyone, prepare to evacuate at a moment’s notice. The retreat’s auto defenses will take care of the rest. We don’t have to be here for the house to kick some serious ass. We can monitor from the sub and accelerate any action we deem necessary. Mum will grab all our kits. Everyone be on standby for a potential deployment." Tim commanded.

We were about two miles from the coast and the subterranean river would enable us to escape undetected. I hoped this was a false alarm I thought to myself as I headed to Potts' sleeping area. Michelle joined me looking a little anxious.

"You okay, baby?"

"Yes, Todd. We thought DM was getting close, but this could be an all-out assault to try and retrieve William and his device. Believe me when I tell you, DM is a very serious threat. They will come with guns blazing and no regard for casualties other than William." was Michelle's guarded reply.

Suddenly I was pissed off. Part of me wanted to stay and fight and kick some ass. The smarter part of me knew Potts and his invention was too important to let fall into the wrong hands. Do your job and trust the training. As we followed Tim's instructions, I could only imagine what was going on just off property. I hoped nothing.

I scanned the sky with my binoculars, fruitlessly hoping we hadn't been detected. "Son of a bitch, they launched a drone. They must have seismic detectors. Damn thing will surely be infrared capable. Everyone here?" I asked.

"All here, Sam." George replied, "We got about twelve minutes before the drone sweeps our position. As much as I would like to go in quiet, we are way past that shit. We need to hit them hard and fast. Send a bunker buster into the garage pad and we should be able to rappel down from there. The house defenses will be good. We can deploy some chaff, and it should engage the lasers long enough for us to gain entry to the house. Timing will be crucial, as the chaff and the missile need to arrive at the same time. So, we need to be about thirty seconds behind the explosion. We will have one shot at this, and if we fuck it up, people won't be going home tonight."

Like I said before, she's fucking brilliant.

"All right, send the exact coordinates to the ship and have them give us a count. Tell them to blanket the house with three chaff bombs and make sure the timing is good. Get everyone into the choppers and ready to go. This is going to be tight." I said as we headed to the choppers.

"Where is everybody, Mum?" Catherine barked as she and Josh exited the Range Rover and ran to join us.

"I'm grabbing our kits. Tim is setting the house for defense and monitoring the drone's progress. Todd and Michelle are with William." I replied, exiting Elle.

"Okay, send a rally call to everyone and get them down here. DM is about a click away and they have a light destroyer offshore that can make our day problematic." Catherine instructed.

A soft alarm rang throughout the house. Michelle and I grabbed Potts and headed to the elevator. As we approached the elevator, the lights in the house went red, and we knew the perimeter defenses had been activated. Thumper joined us, handing out weapons. He grabbed Potts and ushered him to the elevator.

"We got maybe six short ones before all bloody hell breaks loose. Stoppin' at the garage and pickin' up

Catherine and me mate, then down to the sub." Thumper told us.

When Elle arrived at the garage level, we felt a thump and saw a flash just as the doors opened. The concussion of the blast hurled Catherine forward in midair towards the opening of the elevator. Without thinking, I crouched and caught her limp body like a catcher receives a fastball. Thumper dashed out towards Josh who was limp and bleeding in the middle of the floor. He immediately sent a spray of lead towards the opening of the garage. He got Josh to the elevator and the door began to close. I glimpsed DM for the first time. In black camo, rappelling down from hovering choppers, they hit the opening like a well-oiled team.

"Danger close, Charlie one." Thumper yelled.

As the doors closed, I could see streams of foam coming from everywhere, starting to solidify. Looking down, I realized Catherine and Josh needed first aid and they needed it now! As we started down to the sub, I could only wonder what was going on just a few yards away. The foam looked like it might slow them down.

My teams were in the choppers. The missile had launched from the destroyer offshore. It looked like our timing might just work, I thought to myself. We came in low and fast. As the chaff exploded over the estate the lasers engaged. There must have been six or seven of them firing in random patterns. They were well placed and would have been devastating if we hadn't sent the aerial bombs. As the bunker buster hit the slab, it went up in a huge fireball and debris flew everywhere. The house visibly shuddered, but no damage that we could see other than the slab disintegrating. As we started to rappel down, the electronics in the chopper began to go nuts.

"Put this bitch on the ground. We just got hit with an EMP pulse" I screamed at the pilot. The choppers immediately went to auto gyro, and we descended fast and hard. As we hung from the rappel lines, it was all we could do to keep out of the way of the choppers. In just a few seconds all three choppers were on the ground, the electronics fried. That crazy bitch never ceased to amaze me. A directional pulse gun that could disable electronics. She was really beginning to piss me off.

“Everybody, attack formation Delta. Hit the garage deck and let’s close before they can escape.” Augustus yelled.

As expected, George was the first to breach the opening, and after a quick survey he headed to the elevator. Someone was pulling a wounded man towards the it, and as he did, he sent a very accurate spray of machine pistol fire George’s way. Damn that friggin’ guy was good. One man down, and George ducked for cover. “Team two, cover and move.” he shouted.

A fine spray of foam began to cover everything. It began to harden on contact and made movement almost impossible. And just like that it was over.

“Exit to the rear and do it on the quick.” George yelled.

I was really pissed. “Son of a bitch.” I screamed. “She did it again. I can’t believe some of the crazy shit she comes up with.”

As we stood there looking at a wall of foam, we couldn’t believe how fast it activated. In mere minutes it became a wall that would require chainsaws and shovels to get through.

"Bloody hell, boss, SAS is on the way. Maybe fifteen minutes tops, and we have no extraction vehicles." Augustus shot at me.

"I'm on it." George yelled. "Extraction point Echo and a chopper will pick us up. We had two causalities, one to enemy fire and the other to the foam."

She must be very well connected if the SAS is on the way in less than fifteen minutes, I thought. That is a quick response time under any circumstances, let alone as well planned as our attempt was. Hard to believe we didn't even see Potts, or even get a shot at them. We were going to have to step it up if we wanted to derail this team. There must be a grotto or underground river beneath the estate, leading out to sea. "George, send a message to the ship to monitor the coast. With any luck, we will get another shot at them in open water." I ordered as I ran to the extraction point.

Chapter 10 – Recovery

"Get Josh and Cat to the infirmary, Tim." Mum instructed. "Thumper, you take your position at the helm. Todd, are you and Michelle okay?"

"I've got two little shrapnel nicks and a slight concussion, but other than that I'm good to go." I replied.

"Oui, Mum, I am fine. A little dazed and bruised but ready to go." said Michelle.

As Tim took Josh, Mum ordered Thumper to take us out. The sub was automated, and it took very little on our part to get underway. Thumper fired up the H-Drives and we were off.

"Lay in a course to the Denmark location Thumper, and activate the stealth tech. I'm sure DM is scanning the coast as we speak and just looking for an opportunity to take another bloody poke at us. Cheeky bastards." Mum instructed as she picked Cat up and trundled off to the stern of the sub.

I was more than a little worried as I saw Cat motionless in Mum's arms. I suddenly realized with a moment of clarity that I cared for everyone on the team more than ever. I had heard that people connect on a very close level when in a combat situation. I thought it was just bullshit, but now I knew. I hoped she would be okay.

As the sub slipped away from the dock and began to submerge, I couldn't help but think this task was taking on huge proportions. We all saw the potential of William's device, but the reality that someone else knew we had it and would stop at nothing to get it was a sobering thought. I wondered how long we would be at sea.

In front of me were several screens. The one directly in front of me was lit in a soft blue hue, with Thumpers instructions crawling across the screen. I instinctively knew there was to be no talking, and that all conversation was to be exchanged on the screen in front of me. We were in stealth mode, trying to slip away undetected. I couldn't hear a sound as we silently glided along.

I could see the route laid in course and speed. We were doing thirty-five knots, which is really moving underwater. In no time we had breasted the coast and turned north towards Denmark. On the screen in front of me, I could see the ship lying about seven miles off the coast, outside of territorial waters. Thumper had deployed a long-range, high-altitude drone that gave us real time images of our very earnest enemy, DM.

I could tell they didn't yet have a clue that we had entered the ocean. Suddenly three sonic buoys were dropped in a random pattern offshore. They showed up as green dots on my screen. I could almost see Thumper smiling as he typed, "Watch this." It felt like the sub burped and one by one the dots shimmered and disappeared.

"What just happened, Thumper?" I typed on the screen.

"An underwater EMP pulse just smoked all the electronics on their sonic buoys. And the good part is, because of the water density they will never know where the pulses came from. Really cracks my ass up to mess with their heads." Thumper typed in reply.

As we reveled in the amazing gadgets at our disposal Catherine groggily entered the room. She had bandages around her head and her left arm. She looked a little dazed and disorientated but she was vertical. We all let out a collective sigh when we saw not only our leader, but someone who was so close to us all. I started to rise when she put a hand on my shoulder and motioned me to stay. Leaning over, she gave me a soft kiss on the head and did the same for Michelle and Thumper. Typing into the screen she said, “Concussion and some bruising. Josh is in rough shape. Tim and Mum are attending to him. William is safe, resting in a stateroom. He is a little disoriented and a bit overwhelmed. I’ll send Mum to him in a moment. We should be out of the destroyer’s range and be able to surface in a few hours. I’m sure everyone could use some fresh air. We have a lot to talk about. When we get everyone stable and out of danger we will meet in the mess. Thumper, I’ll take the helm. Would you go make us some food? Suddenly I’m famished.”

I realized how hungry I was. I could hardly wait for Thumper to get back from the mess with some chow.

“How bad is Josh hurt?” I typed to Cat.

“It’s not good. Spleen has a small tear in it and both lungs are bruised. Right arm and right leg are broken, and he has a concussion. No cranial bleeding that we can detect, but he is in rough shape. Mum could almost operate and repair his spleen, but we need an anesthesiologist to monitor his vitals. He is in stable but in critical condition. We carry typed and cross-matched blood for all team members. It will take us about twelve hours at flank speed to get to our destination. We need to surface soon as we can, we will make better time on the surface." Catherine replied.

Thumper walked in with several trays loaded with sandwiches, fruit and some vegetable snacks.

"Here you go blokes. Enjoy. Cat, I'm going back to the infirmary to check on me mate." Thumper said in a quiet whisper.

"I understand, Thumper. I think we are out of range and can resume normal operations." she said as she wearily sat down in the captains' chair. The drone has the destroyer about thirty miles south of us. We will run for another hour underwater and then surface. I don't think their radar can reach past seventy miles. It's not the most advanced ship in their fleet. Although she is a sea-worthy older Vietnam War era destroyer, from what we can tell she is not yet outfitted with the latest tech. We will try to get to a shipping lane and run next to some friendly tankers in the area. That will minimize the satellite's ability to register us. I'm not sure if they have the electronic signature of this ship, but they will before the day is out." Catherine responded.

Chapter 11 – Pursuit

I was not amused by any means. We had just lost a man; three helicopters and we didn't get to Potts. As my team and I landed on the aft deck of the destroyer, I knew I was going to catch it in a moment. My boss was not used to me failing and neither was I. He would have more than a few questions. They were so prepared for us. We need to catch them in the open where we can maximize our potential for success. Son of a bitch, that was close. Just sixty seconds and I think we would have had Potts in hand and most of their team dead or incapacitated. That foam was incredible, I thought to myself. It was a clever breach defense. We should look at integrating it into our defensive systems. I climbed towards the bridge, rehearsing what I was going to say. As always, I would just deliver the facts.

The captain motioned to me as I entered the bridge. "Conference Skype call in my stateroom in five minutes." he instructed.

Augustus walked onto the bridge." The blokes want a bit of chow and some first aid. Debrief first or chow and patch them up?"

“Take care of their immediate needs, and we will debrief them later.”

“You got it Gov. See you in a bit.” Augustus said as he exited the room.

“Captain, do we have a satellite link yet, so we can look for the sub?” I said pacing back and forth on the bridge.

“Not yet Sam, but we should have one in about an hour and be able to sweep the area. Do you have any idea what sector they might be in?”

“Well, the damn buoys were of no use, but I think they would have headed south. More shipping channels and some sub pack bases to the south. It would give them a better chance to blend in with some other ship traffic. However, the Russians and the Brits both have naval bases to the north and their sub would fit right in. I think they may be using a new propulsion system, a hydrogen drive, hybrid of sorts. If they are, we will get very little heat signature. We need to look for displacement in a seventy-mile radius. It will take a while, but we need to develop a profile of their sub for our files and find them at all costs.” I said earnestly.

"Agreed, Sam. I will make it so. Your conference call is ready. Good luck!" the captain informed me.

"Thanks, it's all good. No one thought this would be easy, least of all Yong Pak. See you in a bit." And with that I walked into the captain's stateroom and fired up the screen.

"Hello, Mr. Pak."

"Let's discuss your recent failure, shall we?" Yong said.

Chapter 12 – Evasion

We had been running on the surface for five hours and were making great time. I was standing watch on the weather deck with a pair of military grade binoculars scanning the horizon. It seemed silly as the detection tech could spot a fly at a thousand meters and tell you what color his eyes were. But I liked the nostalgic feel of standing watch on a sub. There was something soul inspiring, looking at the ocean's horizon as you move through the water.

At this speed we would arrive in about six hours, give or take. We all had gone in to see Josh, and he was in bad shape. Catherine was in constant communication with the next retreat, giving instructions for our arrival. Potts was with her also making requests. Something was up, and I was pretty sure it had to do with Josh. Mum had done an amazing job. I thought she had probably been a trauma nurse or maybe even a surgeon in a past life. Josh was resting in a chemical induced coma, and between the monitors and the IV lines, he looked like a pincushion.

Michelle came through the hatch and gave me a warm hug. "Go below Todd and I will take the next watch."

With that, I headed below and took my position at the dive controls. Thumper was at the helm, and we were alone in the control room.

"How you holdin' up, big guy?" I asked.

"Not too bad, mate. Worried about me mate. Josh is as tough as they come, and he will bloody well make it if anyone can. I think that Mum, Cat and Potts are cooking something up, and it may have something to do with Josh. I hope so 'cause he is in bad nick right now and could use a hand up."

"Well, if anyone could put together a good outcome, I trust that group over any other."

"I agree, and we will know in a short one. You will like the next retreat. I've only been once me self, but from what I remember it's quite the flat. It's an old Russian sub pen, complete with bombproof doors. The inside's modeled after a futuristic space outpost, very high tech for the day, and enclosed completely in the mountain. With the tech we have, you would never know where it was or that it even existed unless you were to follow us directly in. It's a nice place to lay me head and a good place for Josh to get some proper care."

"I've yet to be somewhere with this group that is not just first class all the way."

"Sure mate."

Chapter 13 – Accountability

"Well, Mr. Craze, would you care to enlighten me on your recent attempt to deliver what you have promised me?" asked Yong Pak.

"You know as well as I do, sir. We were transmitting in real time all that took place while we attempted to breach their defenses. You were able to witness their defenses and the timing of it all. Even you must agree we were only off by maybe sixty seconds or so. From George's cam, it looked like Catherine was banged up and one of her men, too. I think the big guy's name is Thumper, and he's very good. We got a partial of the new man and are running it through the files now. I don't think we will find him in our database as she is very good at hiding identities. We did get them on the run, and it will take a while before they return to that facility, if ever. Our best chance is to catch them in the open and take a shot at them when the odds are a bit more in our favor." I replied with a hint of sarcasm.

"It would appear she is a bit more challenging an adversary than you will admit. Perhaps I have assembled the wrong team for this particular mission."

"Mr. Pak, you can do whatever you want to as far as the team is concerned. But if you think I will stand idle and listen to you impugn my character and my intentions, you are very wrong. My services are in high demand, and if you say the word I can be gone tomorrow. Then, good luck finding and catching Potts. You should have stuck with him at MIT when you had the chance. What's your decision sir?"

"No need to be so upset. You Americans are so defensive. My questions are well founded, and I am but searching for an answer to my problem. How to secure my former lab mate, as you so aptly reminded me, and the technology we both developed. My inspiration was a large part of the success of the device. However, Potts had the imagination of a brilliant mind and could think well outside the box. If I could but talk to him for a moment, I know I could assist him with his vision for his device. Between us we could reshape mankind's future. So please, Mr. Craze, continue your pursuit of Mr. Potts and keep me advised of your progress." Pak said with a typical oriental assertive calm.

On that note he signed off. The prick always managed to get the last word. If he didn't pay so extraordinary well, he could kiss my ass. It sounded like the device Potts developed was a bit more groundbreaking than Pak first let on. It would be nice to know what it did and how much it might be worth. Shape the world? Pak was one crazy fuck. People like him always freak me the hell out. World domination and all that crap I don't buy it and don't want it. Do my job, get paid and move on. After this one maybe retire and play golf somewhere. Arizona sounds good. Be nice to quit chasing Catherine all over the damn globe. Shit, I must be getting old and soft. Last one I think -- last mission. I'm done.

"Damn, is this the best we can fuckin' do?" I screamed. "With all this technology at our disposal, we can't find one damn sub in less than 10,000 square miles of ocean? We can find a cow in Canada with hoof and mouth disease out of thousands and this escapes us? Dammit!"

"Hey boss, give this a look." Augustus pointed at the screen. "I think I've found the bloody thing."

“I hope like hell you have; I’m losing my mind over this one.”

“Well, take a look at this. It looks like a magma displacement of some sort. I’ve seen whale signatures before and it looks the same only bigger. Bloody hell, look at the wake signature, very little thermal signature but definitely displacing water. It’s in about the right place, too. Looks like she’s headed to Norway or maybe Denmark.”

“Good work, Augustus. Here is what I want to do. Find their yacht that sailed out of Dubrovnik. See where the hell it went, and if there is a captain or any crew aboard get them. Bring them to me, and let’s see if we can convince them to talk.” I’m sure George can, as that seems to give him great pleasure, I thought.

“Captain, put us in the wind, and let’s launch the helicopter and go find some intel. In the meantime, we shall steam for Denmark.”

As I stood on the bridge, I realized she was always one step ahead of me. I wondered if I had someone on my team feeding her info. Just doesn’t seem possible. Damn if she doesn’t seem to have twenty-third century tech. I was beginning to think she wasn't from around here. As I walked to the fantail of the ship, I thought to myself. If she went to Denmark and had found an old sub pen to hide in, it was going to be tough to find her. The Russians built those as almost indestructible, and with her stealth tech and ability to fortify her location, it would be tough to find and to mount an attack. Our best bet was to catch her in the open, but we needed to find her first and wait until she fucked up. I still wasn't too crazy about Yong and his crazy ass scheme to take over the planet. I don't know a lot about Potts or what he put together, but with the amount of money being spent to find it, it must be something special.

Perhaps I should talk to the guys to create our own mission and maybe negotiate a better deal, I thought to myself. Although I knew that Pak would pay me and the team eleven million if we were successful. But if he would part with eleven so easily, it must have been worth hundreds of millions. I think Augustus would go for it and the other seven guys would, too. George, I'm not so sure about—I thought maybe he was here to keep an eye on us. I would hate to take that bastard on, it would take a tank to take him out.

Chapter 14 - The Miracle

"Prepare to dock." Thumper instructed from the helm, as we surfaced and came to a stop. I admired the location. We were just outside of Aarhus Denmark. It was an old, converted sub pen used by the Russians in the cold war. Long abandoned, Catherine converted the existing structure into something out of a science fiction movie. We had entered the dock under water, and from the monitor we could see what looked like a wall of rock and stone climbing several hundred feet straight from the sea's edge. Thumper had told me, the tech here was even more sophisticated than the other sites. The stone face on the outside was a holographic projection that disguised any irregularities of the bluff's face.

From the outside you had no indication, except for a small heat signature, that anything out of the ordinary existed here. But the inside was a technological marvel. As we came to rest, several men tethered the boat to the dock. We exited the conning tower and walked down the gangway to the dock. Several men with a hard board and a gurney were on the way below decks to retrieve Josh and take him to the ICU. We had not had a meeting as Catherine and Mum had been engaged with William the entire length of our journey from England.

The walls of the sub pen on the inside were coated with a synthetic foam that assumed the shape of the rock, but with no musty odor and the temperature felt perfect even around the water. Moisture rose from the water, as the air temp was warmer than the liquid below. Ducting fans along the dock pulled all the moisture away from the equipment and material staged along the dock. The lighting was a soft green, and we could see very well. The lighting enhanced your eye's ability to focus.

Mum motioned for us to follow her towards the elevator. As we entered, Elle said, "Hello, Todd. What floor may I take you to?" Mum answered, "Fifth floor, please." Turning to me, she said "We are going straight to the conference room to have a chat. Everyone will be there including a few of our team you ain't met yet. Catherine and William will join us in a bit. Josh, me precious luv, is being taken to the infirmary. Our resident surgeon has been flown in to attend to him. We will know of his condition in a little while."

As we exited Elle and entered the conference room, I let out an exclamation of wonder. Before us was something straight out of a Star Trek episode. The walls looked like mirrors, and the ceiling was made of transparent fabric that moved in a wave. I couldn't tell if it was real or an optical illusion. The lighting was the same green as at the dock, and the air felt oxygen enriched. I was more alert, and the fatigue of the last few days was not as noticeable.

"Everyone, grab a seat." Mum directed.

The table was a grayish, glass affair that appeared to be suspended in midair. The chairs were simple in structure with high backs and a supple leather fabric covering them. As I sat, a screen and keyboard lit up under the surface of the table. Across the screen the words select temperature and comfort setting appeared. There was a firmness setting on the touch screen, and you slid your finger along the bar graph until the desired setting was reached. Another bar controlled the seat's temperature and a third the lighting of the screen imbedded in the tabletop. This was some crazy tech, and as a computer guy, I loved it. I had seen some prototypes of this technology, but nothing in practical application.

As we all sat marveling at the new toys, Catherine and William entered the room with three strangers.

"It is very good to see everyone in such good spirits after what we have been through. I will answer your questions at the end of this briefing. Let me start by saying thank you to everyone for the quick and professional response at the Retreat outside of London. That was very close. Just sixty seconds separated DM from success and us from potential mortal harm. Josh is severely injured, and we are considering using Williams' device to pull him through." she said with mixed emotions.

We all began to speak at once, and Cat raised her hands to quiet us down.

"We have spent the last six hours with William discussing this and believe we have come to a safe and perhaps lifesaving conclusion. Josh's lungs are failing. The bruising was too severe from the concussion of the blast. We are keeping the clotting at bay with blood thinners, but without a new lung he won't survive the week. The doctor is attending to him as we speak and confirming our diagnosis. If he concurs with our assessment of Josh's condition, we will perform an intervention in thirty-six hours or less, depending on how long it takes for William and his team to set up the device. The site we are in is almost undetectable and we are as safe as is humanly possible in today's world." she said with an air of reserved calm.

"I would like you to meet some of the blokes at this Retreat." Mum said as she stood. The cheeky man on the right is Artevius Goodson. The luv with the bright red hair is the house mum, Maria Poplov and her blond mate, Heidi Larrsen. You will get to know them all a bit better in the days and weeks to follow. We currently have thirteen tuff soldiers with a variety of skills to help us. All of them are like me children. Give each one of them the love and respect I do."

As everyone exchanged pleasantries and sat back down, we all turned our focus back to Catherine.

"Well, it is no secret that DM is after William and FEAT. They will expend every effort and spare no expense to secure both items. We will stay at Alert 2 for as long as we are here. Our movements have been monitored by more than DM, and other governments are more than a little suspicious as to our intentions. I have been in contact with several heads of state to identify our intentions and to assure them we mean no harm. The last thing we need is attempted military intervention. I have attempted to calm them and let them know that we are nothing more than a think tank with some exotic lab locations. So far so good, as most seem to be buying it. Our problem is many-fold. The device works. The world will never be the same. If our intervention with Josh works, immortality may become a reality. I don't need to tell all of you the panic and fear that would be set in motion if this were known. The powers of the world would stop at nothing to get it. There would not be a safe place on Earth to hide. Our quest is to develop the device to its potential and discover a way to launch it to the world that will not create a total collapse of life as we know it. It's going to be difficult. Our biggest and perhaps safest ally would obviously be the United States. They have the military capacity and enough hardened sites that we could be protected from anything short of a thermonuclear event. I am in contact with a very select group in the US intelligence community. We had our new friends run a sweep of our general location, and they could not detect us. If they can't find us, it's a safe guess no one else can." she said with more than a little fear in her voice.

"This new information has a set of dynamics I don't think anyone was prepared for. Immortality! Really, when William and I met, we considered many possibilities, but believe me, that was not one of them. With that said, we would like everyone to get something to eat and get some rest. Will everyone please wear their Suit tonight, as there is a good bit of information that you need to acquire in a short time. I know you have a million questions, and by morning most of them will have been answered. Get some rest, thank you, and sweet dreams." She sat down quietly with an exhausted sigh.

"Okay, me lovelies, off to the pantry and let's have a bit of food. Maria has prepared some lovely food for us. Then off to bed, and we will shake it back here at eight." Mum softly directed.

Catherine motioned for me to come speak with her. “Todd, would you come see me in my room after you’ve eaten?” she softly requested.

“Sure, as soon as I get a bite, I’ll head your way.”

She gave me a one-armed hug. “Great.” was her soft reply.

The next hour was filled with speculation and wonder. Each of us was smart enough to know we were involved in something that was life altering. Immortality seems like a science fiction dream, but to be in the presence of a device that could deliver it was more than my brain could wrap itself around. To think, short of an accident, one could live, how long? Possibly six hundred, seven hundred or even one thousand years? Could our brains handle the stress of that? From my readings of the bible, it had been possible at one time. Men and women had lived well beyond six hundred years before “the Great Flood.” So, if you believe in that, it wasn’t too far out of the question to think we might have figured out how to do it again.

As we all speculated on the enormity of the moment, there was a guarded exuberance. To not have to worry about illness or sickness, to be as healthy as we were when we were twenty-five would be exhilarating. The possibilities were endless, not only from an intellectual perspective, but from a spiritual place as well. How great would it be for mankind to realize its full potential and to experience so much life? The thought was a heady one. Having talked with everyone and finished my meal, I said my goodnights and headed to Cat's room. Michelle gave me a soft nod and a wink as I left. She was engaged with Heidi, and they seemed like lifelong friends. Somehow, I think she knew where I was going and approved.

I walked towards Catherine's room, which I assumed would be in the same place as all the other retreats. I was close. The halls were of the same material as the conference area. Soft music was playing, and the same green hue was everywhere. I liked the effect the light had on my vision; it was soothing to my tired eyes. As I approached a door the wall came alive. A picture of a country scene appeared, and the name Catherine Bushnell appeared above the door.

The door opened with a soft whoosh, and I stepped inside. Everything was a pastel white with the ever-present green lighting overhead. The walls were rounded and looked supple to the touch. All the furnishings were modular and looked like they just came out of a Deep Space Nine set. Catherine walked out of what I assumed was the bathroom in a rose-colored sheer robe. She was stunning, and I could tell she needed comfort. I moved towards her and took her in my arms. She let out a sigh.

"Will you spend the night with me, please" she whispered into my neck.

"Yes." I whispered back.

"Would you like to shower?"

"I would, and Mum asked us to wear our Suits to-night."

"I know, I had your Suit and bed sent here. After a bit, we can both retire to our beds, but I would like to spend some time with you first."

For the first time she sounded vulnerable to me, and I realized the enormity of the moment was taking its toll on even her.

"That sounds nice. Do you have some brandy or anything to drink? I suddenly have the urge for a stiff one."

The shower felt good as I washed away the events of the last few days. It just felt good in its simplicity, and with a good meal in me I felt both relaxed and happy. The recent conversations would find their way back into the forefront of my thinking, but for now, some light conversation, the touch of a woman, and a strong drink were simple needs, but perfect.

I walked back into the sitting area with a towel wrapped around me, and she came to me, drink in hand. What a rare human being, so full of life and the sense of a greater responsibility. With her wealth she could go anywhere, do anything and travel in circles only the top one percent could. To her credit, she had devoted herself to the furthering of humanities journey with all its quirky and sometimes very dark behavior. As she handed me a drink, I noticed a tenderness in her eyes I had seen only a time or two before. I selfishly hoped it was for me. Her hand slid to the small of my back and she pulled me close. The scent of her was intoxicating, and I felt myself inwardly moan as all the possibilities flashed in my mind's eye.

She looked up at me and asked, “Will you make love to me?”

Without a word, I took the glass from her hand and set them both on the small table in front of us. Reaching under her, I lifted her off her feet and slowly began to kiss her moist, exquisite lips. As I carried her towards the bed my towel slipped off, and she ran her hand down the small of my back, cupping my firm cheek in her long fingers. A moan escaped us both as we felt the delicious contact. With her cradled in my arms, I turned my back to the bed. Slowly sitting down, I continued my wet embrace of her sweet lips. I rolled onto my back moving her on top of me as our kiss continued. Pulling away from my mouth, she rose to her knees and removed the robe. Her body was so perfect. Her proportions were what I liked. Smallish waist, very full athletic hips and full breasted. Not to mention just under the skin a feeling of muscularity. And the soft downy hair all over her body never ceased to arouse me. I had to mentally pinch myself to even begin to believe I was here at this moment in time with this beautiful woman who had somehow chosen me.

My hands glided on her soft skin, exploring every inch of her. There was urgency in her look as if she needed to be taken, softly, yet with conviction. My arousal was obvious and soon we were in a lovers' embrace. I pulled her towards me, we rolled over, intertwined together in a blissful connection. Soon we were in the deep throes of lovemaking, oblivious to anything other than the moment. With a loud groan we rode the wave of pleasure and were soon spent and exhausted. Spooning her from behind, I softly whispered. "I love you, Catherine Bushnell." I felt her melt into me as she pulled my arms closer in an even tighter embrace.

And with that we chatted for a few moments, donned our suits, climbed into our beds and drifted off to a much needed rest.

Precisely at eight, everyone assembled in the conference room. Mum was at the head of the table and asked us to direct our attention to the wall behind her. The wall suddenly came alive with a map of the area. The same map was displayed on the screen before us on the table.

With a laser cursor in his hands, Thumper directed our attention to Denmark.

"We are approximately here." he said, pointing to a section of the coast. "The last known coordinates of DM were here." he pointed to a section of ocean just outside of London. "We now know they have attempted to track us with not only satellite but drone tech. We're not sure they have succeeded, but we must be ready for anything. Cat has been in touch with our new allies the United States. I love those Yanks. Even you Todd." Everyone chuckled. "If we can get ourselves safely from here to Aberdeen by sub then a transport plane will take us to a hardened facility in the Casper Mountain range of Wyoming. Mum, do you have something for us?" Thumper asked in a serious tone.

"Yes, my dear. At precisely two p.m. today Josh will undergo a treatment from FEAT. William has assured us the outcome will be nothing less than brilliant. Let us all take a moment when we can and wish him well. He is still unconscious and won't be awake until right before the procedure. We will roust him long enough to tell him what we are about to do and make sure he agrees with us. My lovely Josh will soon be in good nick and back with us." Mum said as a small tear slid down her rosy cheek.

William stood and walked to the front of the room with what appeared to be a giant ball of fur. Looking rested and very excited. He always seemed to be very excited.

"Meet Sweetness, our resident cat. She is a healthy Main Coon of five years. She inadvertently was subjected to FEAT when we were perfecting it in the UK. We thought the lab had been sealed but she had hidden under a section of cabinets. The good news is she is fine. The more interesting news is that after careful examination we have concluded that all cellular degradation has ceased, and her cells are replicating at an astonishing rate. No disease or muscle wear or effects of aging are present. We believe the effect will last indefinitely, and short of an accidental termination she could live well into the hundreds. From what we can tell the cellular excitation at the DNA level will last between six and seven hundred years in humans. She has helped guide our decision to use the device on Josh. We will revive Josh from his coma and tell him of our intentions. With his permission, we will introduce the effects of FEAT to his cells. I know the ramifications are very troubling, but I have invested my life into doing what I think is right. If we are good stewards of this technology, mankind can enter an era of enlightenment never seen before. I want to thank you for your support, and Catherine for her steadfast vision of my work and her willingness to protect me and FEAT at all costs. I will do all that I can to maintain your trust and your respect." William said with a profound air of conviction.

We all stood and gave this tousled-haired Einstein a rousing round of applause and accolades. One by one we approached him with hugs, handshakes or kisses, as gender dictated. We all were so proud of him and his unselfish humble stature. Catherine was beaming with pride and looked so hopeful for mankind's future.

"Ok everyone, let's go to the surgical theater. Those that don't want to may go to their respective posts and we will see everyone a little later." said Catherine with an air of expectation and hope.

We entered the sitting area around the surgical theatre. William, Mum and someone who must have been the doctor were at Josh's bedside. Josh slowly became awake, and we could sense his distress. His lungs were barely functioning, and at this rate, it wouldn't be long before he was unable to sustain life. We could see Mum bend over to him and talk into his ear. He had a breathing tube in place and was unable to verbally respond. After a moment we saw two quick nods and he visibly relaxed. Mum gave him a tender kiss on his forehead, and with that, she left the room. The doctor sat on a stool behind a screen at Josh's side. FEAT was placed vertically with the small rod over Josh. Everything else looked the same as the first demonstration. Potts sat at the laptop and began to direct the machine. The lights dimmed slightly as it came up to full power. A reddish glow emanated from the device, and it slowly swept from Josh's toes to his head and then back. There was a light humming sound as it passed over his body, and other than the soft red light, nothing. No loud noise, no flashing lights, no bells. It was almost anticlimactic. And then, Josh's skin began to glow a soft pink, and his breathing slowly returned to a normal rhythm. On the monitors you could see his vital signs improving dramatically, and the doc gave a big "thumbs" up, and a smile.

"This will take about three hours as near as we can tell from the limited experience we have. But we will know very soon if this has been in Josh's best interest. We will let you know if there is any change." William informed us through the theatre's sound system.

With that, we all went to various parts of the facility to prepare for the day and train for anything else that might come up. I couldn't help but think we had just witnessed the next step in mankind's journey. What a great responsibility we all now collectively shared. I hoped we were up to the task.

Chapter 15 – The Day After

I walked into the mess hall and saw only Michelle at a table. “Where is everybody?” I asked.

“Good morning luv, how are you? Everyone is still waking up. Mum said to wait here until everyone has arrived. Let’s eat.” said Michelle.

“Okay, baby, but are you good? The suit kicked my butt last night, and I’m not only starving but exhausted. That was a lot of information last night, and it always kicks my ass a little for the first few hours after I wake.”

“Make a hole, ya bloody mutt. Make room for a bloke who needs a bit of chow.” boomed Thumper as he sauntered into the room.

And then the flash mob descended. A throng of people entered the mess hall, all talking at once. In the forefront was Josh, who less than twelve hours ago was at death’s door. Michelle jumped up, ran to him and wrapped herself around him like a koala bear. He was the only one not dressed like us. He was in green pajamas of some kind. He did look good though.

"Easy, easy Michelle, I'm not quite ready for the likes of you yet. But hold that thought, as I will be soon." grinned Josh.

If I weren't seeing it with my own eyes, I would call you a liar if you told me he would be up so quick. He looked dang good, no limp of any kind, and all his limbs seemed to be working. From where I was, it looked like he was breathing normally.

"Damn, Josh, how are you feeling?" I asked in amazement.

"Sore as hell, but in good nick, other than that. No, I feel like I could bloody eat a whole cow and half a dozen chickens. Let me at the food."

"Hello, all my lovelies. How are all my children this morning?" Mum asked as she made her entrance into the room.

All of us shouted our good mornings and hellos in a jubilant chorus, given Josh's obviously most excellent condition.

"A little quiet then, and let's have a bit of chow. William and Catherine will be around in a moment and have a few words for the lot of ya." Mum said with a smile.

Everyone looked so happy to see Josh up and about. With a moment of clarity, I realized I wanted to be next to go under the device and have my life changed forever. As I looked around the room, I wondered who else thought as I did, and who might want a shot at immortality.

Chapter 16 – Interrogation

"The trick is to find out what terrifies ya. Everyone has something. Da not care how tuff you thin' ya are, ya got somethin'. This nasty one here is pretty tuff but we found his tickle." George beamed. "Ya would not guess it but this tuff boy don like his eyes fucked with. Beat his ass pretty good and used some pentothal on him but when I put the cold laser to his eyes 'e sang like a three-year-old."

"Who the hell is he, George?" I asked.

"One of the tuffs on the yacht. He has told us all he knows, believe me. I can smoke him if ya like." George smiled with a happy grin.

"Naw, let's wait a bit until we get to where were going. He might still be of some help to us. What's his name?"

"Peter Taylor, from South Africa. Wanna know his kids' names, wife, best friends and a bunch of other useless crap? I got gigs and gigs of vocal on this one." George said.

"Will he continue to talk?"

"Oh, hell ya, won't ya, tuff." asked George.

A timid and terrified "Yes." was his reply.

"Where are Catherine and her team?"

"Denmark." Peter replied.

"Do you know exactly where?"

"I know she's in an old, converted, Russian sub pen close to Aarhus Denmark. I don't have the coordinates or the exact location. I do know that it's heavily fortified and would take a very focused attack to get them out of there. They could last for a couple of years and stand everything short of a nuclear attack." Peter wearily stated.

"Do you have any way to contact them?"

"My new rally point was Venice, and I was to stay with the yacht until new orders were issued. I'm only the ship's engineer."

"Bullshit, dude. You are a hardened tuff just like us." boomed George. "Da not make me get me shit out again."

"Okay, how else can I help?" Peter weakly replied.

"Stay conscious until I need you. Captain, make our heading to the shores of Denmark, and Augustus search the database for any info on World War Two sub pens in the area." I instructed.

"You got it mate, back to you in a bit." Augustus said as he headed to the com room.

"Peter, can you give me a good reason why I should not let George take you out?" I asked.

"Of course, I can." Peter said with a note of exhaustion in his voice. " Like you, I work for money and will work for the highest bidder. I was the ships engineer on Obsession and one of the defense crew. I have knowledge about their operation and how they cloak their location. And it doesn't matter what George does, my Nimmrod protocol will never allow it to surface unless I make a conscious effort to do so. If the pain becomes too great, my brain will self-terminate before disclosing what I know. So, take me as an ally or kill me—at this point I don't much care either way."

"No fucking way boss. I got every little bit of shit his puny brain could spit out. I know it." George fumed as he closed in on Peter.

"Ease up and give me a minute. You are very good at what you do but his answer makes a lot of sense. Don't you remember how some of Catherine's staff we captured died for no apparent reason? I bet it's exactly what he is talking about." I replied. "So, tell me, Peter, why should I believe you?"

"Good question, and I don't pretend to know it all as my security level was a 7. I was not part of the inner circle. But I know enough to get you close and can tell you more than you will get in the next week on your own."

"Okay, as a show of good faith, give me a piece of intel I don't have, and we will continue our conversation. Fuck with me, and our dear friend George gets to have his way."

"The reason I can only give information voluntarily is the direct result of a device we call Nimmrod. We put on a suit and Nimmrod feeds us info while we sleep. It protects our neural pathways from drugs and torture that might cause us to divulge sensitive material to anyone. I know more about each one of you than you will ever know about me. All the Team has a Suit in each retreat location and can have new info downloaded into their memory every day."

That explained a lot, she seemed to always be one step ahead of me. Every time I moved it was as if she had already successfully predicted my next move. I wondered how I could get my hands on one of those suits.

"Okay, you have my interest. How can I get a suit and get connected?" I asked.

"That's the beauty of Nimmrod, you can't. Unless you are in the control room, and they have set one up for you. If you tried to put anyone else's on, it would be like sticking a live electrical wire into water with the other end in your mouth, a short circuit."

"Okay, let's say for a minute I'm interested in keeping you around. What can you do for us that we can't do for ourselves?"

"I can give you a good idea of the sub pens location and some basic Intel. After that, it's up to you."

"Let me beat it out of him, boss, I'll make him talk. Piece of lying shit pisses me off." screamed George as he clenched and unclenched his fists in anticipation. "Fucking Neanderthal."

"George, you are making this way too fucking personal. Go below and see how the men are doing. I will call you if I need you." I said with a hint of irritability.

The big SOB steamed out of the room, and I knew I would not want to tangle with the guy. Two shots to the head might be a good way to end our friendship.

"How are you able to pull up and override the neural implants?"

"I'm not sure. I think maybe there was a glitch in Nimmrod at the time, and the override protocol was not initiated. For some reason I can pull up anything I want, up to my last download, without hitting a blank. I've never told anyone this 'cause I know they would have corrected it if they knew." Peter stated with a faraway look in his eyes.

"Who is the new guy?"

"Todd Peters. The new golden child. And let me tell you he is freaky good. He took care of the three men in the boat so fast me and Michelle never even raised our weapons. Six rounds, two shots each, three dead, from about sixty yards in the dark. Now that is a freak of nature. No one does that."

"Okay, here is the deal. You stay with us until we breach their defenses or make an assault on their boat, and we will let you go. Or you can join us, and I will give you one of the dead men's share and we will see where it goes."

"Give me a gun."

As I handed him my Glock, I thought to myself, you idiot, you just handed the enemy a loaded weapon. But I felt I had to trust him somehow, and he would never get off the boat alive if he smoked me. As he pulled the slide back and looked to see if there was a round chambered, I held my breath. Smiling, he took aim, spun the weapon in his hand and handed me the gun butt first.

"Tell me what I can do, Sam, and let's go get those crazy sons of bitches." Peter smiled as he handed me back the weapon.

Chapter 17 – Deception

As Catherine entered the mess hall; she looked happy and somber at the same time. "Attention everyone, I need to give you an update. Welcome back, Josh and, believe me, we are all very happy to see you awake and doing so well. The device has performed much better than we had anticipated. William, Mum and I are ecstatic with the results. William is analyzing the data from FEAT."

We all sat in rapt attention. No one moved; we hung on her every word. She looked damn good this morning.

"Josh is healing at a phenomenal rate, and in a few days, we will have good baseline information. With this information, we will try to make intelligent decisions about what to do next. I'm sure we all would like to experience the benefits, and that will be discussed at length very soon. Our immediate goal is to get William and our team safely to a secure site. We are safe here for a little while but eventually people will put two and two together and figure out where we are. There always seems to be someone that sees something. We must protect

William and the device at all costs. We have enlisted the aid of the United States as an ally, and when we are ready, they will aid us in relocating to Wyoming. DM is still actively looking for us, and we believe one of our engineers, Peter Taylor, may have defected. We know he is currently on one of their ships, and they are cruising in our direction. Each of us as a part of Nimmrod has an electronic signature that can be detected from virtually anywhere in the world. If Peter had not defected, he would surely be dead by now." Catherine said with a disappointed sigh.

We all looked at each other shaking our heads. I had liked Peter. He seemed like a straight up guy.

"I believe, and Tim agrees, that we should move to Alert 4 and prepare for evacuation. We probably have about ten hours, give or take. The U.S. will help as soon as we are in international waters, but all hell is going to break loose when we defend ourselves. The international community will demand an explanation. We will not answer until we are secure in the U.S. We want everyone to wear the Suits for the duration of the move. Josh when you feel up to it you need to change."

"William has modified them to act as body shielding. We are going to fit him for one a little later. You can wear clothing or combat gear over them. Some of us will be going to the U.S. and some back to our respective retreats. As a parting thought consider this. You are priority one and will be in the initial control group if you choose. Think long and hard about your decision, as it will affect you for a very long time. Good luck, I love you all, and may God be with us and allow us to serve mankind's best interests." She said this with a little sadness in her voice.

Well, there was the bomb we all had been waiting for. That was it, we were going to the U.S. for aid and shelter. I might have been a little prejudiced, but I think they were the best choice and probably the most capable. As we all split up into groups and began to move towards our assigned areas, Artevius motioned for me to come over to him.

"Todd, we have not had much time to talk but I wanted to thank you for being there for Cat. You remind her of Arthur in some ways, and she gets great comfort from that. He was my best friend, and I have mentored

Cat since she was a young woman. I know you will stand by her and protect her as best you can. Everyone can see you are in love with her, and she loves you also. It is great to see her in love again and beginning to live. Such a tough time for a budding romance to endure, but I believe you two will find a way. Thanks, my friend, and I hope we see each other soon." Artevius said as he embraced me with a very sincere hug.

"I do love her and will do all that I can to shield her from danger." was my reply.

I had no idea her husband's name was Arthur or that his best friend was Artevius. We all loosely said our goodbyes as we broke for different parts of the facility. Josh, Thumper, Mum, Maria and three crew members were in a decoy group headed back to England. Artevius, Heidi and the six of the men originally here were going to stay and defend this position. As soon as we were safely away, they would break in a submarine for Ireland and take a flight to the U.S. Michelle, Tim, Catherine, William and I were going to take the sub out, try to slip up the coast, and then shoot straight for the North Sea.

As soon as we were in international waters, we would have a destroyer escort.

The next few hours were a blur. We loaded all the gear into a small, fast sub that looked like a jet and floated on the water like a boat. We put all of William's gear in a watertight compartment forward and there was still room for the 5 of us if it came down to that. If we came under attack that part of the ship could be detached to float to the surface. William had modified the structural integrity of this vehicle and it would stand a direct hit from almost any conventional weapon.

"Pretty sexy aerosub isn't it?" Tim asked.

"Looks like something out of *Voyage to the Bottom of the Sea."* I replied.

"Dude, it is so much more than that. After Potts got through with it, not much can ding it up. And it is freaky fast, able to do forty-five knots underwater and close to sixty on top of the water. Has the same H-drive as the sub and hardly any signature. Stealthy as all get out. Looks like a dang whale signature underwater when it's moving and shows the displacement signature of a pod of dolphins when it's on top. I tell ya, between Potts and Cat they come up with some cool ass stuff, am I right?" Tim said with a note of pride and some anxiety.

"I'm speechless. Where does she find this stuff?"

"No kidding. Most of it is from people we've helped. Catherine has great vision when it comes to what will work and what won't. Arthur, her husband, was the same. He was brilliant, and one of the classiest guys you would ever meet. Had a knack for getting people to perform way above their comfort zone. Amazing man."

"What happened to him?"

"Run in with DM. Sam Craze got him in a car chase gone wrong." he said as he nervously paced back and forth. I could tell he didn't like remembering this.

"We were helping the man who developed the tech in front of you. He and Arthur were attempting to get to one of the retreats and Sam spotted him. They gave chase and Arthur lost control of the SUV and went right over the edge of a steep embankment. We think Craze shot one or two of the tires out as Arthur was an amazing driver. They died instantly when the car landed and burst into flames. Cat was devastated. You have breathed life back into her, and I want to thank you personally. I know you love her. Hell, everyone knows you love her, and she loves you. Good stuff, brother. Let's load this pig, light the fires and get the hell out of Dodge."

"All right Tim let's do it." I said with some enthusiasm.

The alarm caught us all by surprise. We thought we had a couple more hours. Something must be interfering with Nimmrod's ability to track Peter. Now we just had minutes. The house crew ran to their stations as we boarded the aerosub. I waved goodbye to Mum and her crew as they closed the hatch. Last thing I saw was Thumper smackin' Josh on the butt and giving me a big fist pump. We could hear the defenses powering up. As both subs began to submerge, we started to feel the shudders of rockets hitting the outside of the building. Everyone knew that they could not penetrate the stone or the steel doors protecting the retreat. I hoped the lasers and the rail guns were giving them hell. As we submerged, I sent a silent prayer up to the man and hoped he would watch over us. As we got underway, I was amazed how easy the aerosub was to handle and how gracefully it maneuvered I walked over to Catherine and taking her hand in mine gave it a good squeeze. She smiled and directed me to a dive control panel and weapons screen. All business for now.

"Okay, team, the next few hours are going to be interesting. We are going to slide up the coast of Denmark and when we are at Skagen, we will make a run for it, across the North Sea to Aberdeen. I'm pretty sure they have the signature of the sub we came in on. Let's wish Mum and her team good luck, as they are the decoy. Todd, take the fire control and weapons station. Michelle, take com and radar. Tim, I would like you to take the helm. William, monitor the refinements we made to the ship and document any anomalies. I will monitor the progress of the Denmark Retreat and the location of our decoy. We should just about be exiting the sub pen." As she looked confidently at everyone, she gave us all a thumbs up.

Chapter 18 – Attack

After running for days in this old wore out destroyer we were finally at our destination. Seemed like it took forever to get here, I thought. I just hope Catherine is still where we think she is.

“Okay, here we go. Send the first volley of sidewinders into the face of the cliff. Follow up with a couple of ten inch from the deck guns. In about ten minutes the com is going to be lit up from every international government in a thousand-mile radius.” I said with some concern. “Ignore their demands but be prepared to abandon ship. If they choose to take military action, we will be at their mercy. Put the fast launch in the water and we’ll get the main team on it.” Meaning me and my team. To hell with the rest of them. “The rest of you can defend the ship until you know the end is near. Surrender, and we will take care of the legal as soon as possible. Now hit them again, same sequence. We know they are there, but all we want is for Catherine, Potts and her team to get flushed out. As soon as we detect their magma signature, we will jump into the launch. About three miles away, our sub will surface, and we will get on it. Give chase to their sub and attempt to render it inoperative long enough to get Potts and his invention safely on board." I said with enough conviction to convince those around me.

"The com lines are lighting up, Sam. It won't be long before they'll be all over us." the captain warned.

"I got you. George, you and Augustus take three men and get in the launch. I will be right behind you. Cap, you know what to do. No evidence of us needs to be found, so make sure to clean up any signs we were here before you surrender. Got it?"

"Got it, Sam, and thanks. You and Yong will take care of us, right?" Cap said nervously.

"Absolutely, we won't let you down. Good luck and see you soon." I said with just a trace of sarcasm.

I liked Cap, but sometimes you just can't take any chances. We were in the launch, about a thousand yards away when I keyed the cell. The flash and concussion of the ship going up in flames was deafening. I knew we had ordinance on board, but evidently a bit more than I thought. The concussion wave hit us first and rocked the boat pretty good. I guess I should've felt something about those men. Just didn't; casualties of running with the wrong crowd. I knew I would get "mine" someday and I could bet the bank it wouldn't be pretty.

We saw two jets make a low pass across the ship's burning hull. Secondary explosions rocked the air again as the fuel supply went up. We were a small launch and looked totally civilian. I didn't think anyone would notice us.

Our sub popped to the surface, and we were onboard in two minutes flat and submerged. Before we left the launch, we had opened the seacocks. The launch slipped silently into the deep. Once on board we went straight to the con and began to grab intel on the whereabouts of the bitch and Potts.

"George, you're on weapons, Augustus, I want you on radar and the sat link. I will be at the helm with the Skipper. Report to me directly. Let's move and go get these guys."

"Roger that." said George.

"Bloody hell, right." said Augustus.

The next ten minutes were crucial. We needed to locate them and give chase. We couldn't let them get too far away or we could lose them in the ship traffic.

"Got the bloody bastards in me sights. Give a look Sam, I'm sure it's them. The magma sig matches the one we took the other day. They are on the run for sure. Close to twenty-five knots underwater, and that is haulin'. Not sure we can catch them, but we could send a low yield missile and knock them dead in the water. Almost no loss of life for sure, so no damage to Potts or the rest. Do not care one way or the other, Guvner, but will do what you say." Augustus said with a twisted smile.

"George, what do you think?" Sam asked.

"Blow that bitch up. She ain't so tuff now, is she?"

"You are a ruthless bastard, George. Remind me not to piss you off. Skip, what do we have that can get the job done?"

"Pak sent us a load of weapons before we left and had us load them in a specific pattern. Not sure why, but he said he had good reason. In tube one, we have an electronic signature-seeking missile. Designed as a hull buster, he reconfigured it to deliver a low yield concussion blast and send an EMP pulse that will fry all their electronics and leave them dead in the water. It will go airborne until it's about fifteen hundred meters out then submerge and track until it closes. It's set for a proximity detonation and will go off on its own." the Skipper said.

"Ya know, every once in a while, Pak comes through. How long before we can launch?" I asked.

"About three minutes." George replied.

Chapter 19 – Evasion

As Mum, Josh, Maria and I began to board the sub to head for London, Mum calmly gave us our assignments. “Hello, luv’s. The sub is in good nick and off we go. Josh at the helm. Maria, take the dive planes, and Thumper, you take the radar, sat and weapons.”

I nodded my assent. Mum and I had worked out our logistics days before. She knew I worked best on weapons.

“You other three men know what to do. Two in engineering and the other on com.” She continued “Off ye go now, my lovelies, we are going to head out and kick the dog. Will make for the London retreat as fast as we can go. Apologies all, but we know DM is going to hit us. When we get hit the escape pods are ready to go. Should be a British ship ready to pick us up, and even DM isn’t crazy enough to take on The Royal Navy. Okay, then.” Mum instructed somewhat nervously.

“Hey, Mum, why don’t we sink them first?” asked Josh.

"Well, luv, we want them to think they got us, so Catherine and Potts can get away. If we sink them, they will just send more."

"I get it, Mum, gonna' feed 'em a little blarney." Josh chuckled.

"Naw mate, we're gonna' feed 'em a lot of blarney, and I hope they choke on it." I piped in as everyone chuckled nervously.

"This dang thing is awesome! I feel like we are flying underwater."

"Glad you think so, Todd. A lot of money and research went into this gem of a craft. The original designer was a student of whales, dolphins and barracuda of all things. After studying how they maneuvered in the open ocean he came up with this design. I supplied the funding, and with him and a team of technicians this is the result. We affectionately call it the Manta. The side "wings" will retract when diving and flare out when running the surface. Very fast on the surface, close to sixty knots, which for its size is flying. We are almost 80 feet long and close to 22 feet wide." Catherine explained as she monitored the radar.

"We are ready to make the dash. We will stay under for about one hour, then surface and make our way to Aberdeen. When we surface, we should have a destroyer escort from the U.S., but the international community is not going to be happy with our appearance. We expect DM to mount an assault no matter what the defense looks like. I think we are more than ready for them." she continued.

"Mon cher, are you excited?" Michelle asked.

"Is it that obvious?" was my reply with that ten-year-old grin on my face. Pirates of the North Sea I chuckled to myself.

"I'm excited too." Tim said, batting his eyes in Michelle's direction.

Everyone laughed, and the tension was broken for the moment. We all knew the enormity of the moment and did not take it lightly. But if you can't laugh, what the heck is the reason for living?

"Okay, let's stay focused. The next few hours will ultimately have a profound effect on our future, and we need to be prepared for anything." Catherine said.

We sat in the sub about two miles from where we had assaulted the cliff. I could only guess what was going on in the minds of Catherine's team.

"Hey Sam, look at this, mate. This is the sat image when we assaulted the bunker. Does it look like two subs left when we hit them? The other one is so small it could be a pod of whales scared off by all the activity. I'm not sure what it was mate, but kinda spot on timing if you know what I mean." George queried as he looked at the sat images of the last hour.

"Damn if I know, George. But you are right, it's very strange timing. Do you think they sent a decoy and one or the other is the real target?"

"It's what I would do. The bitch is smart and will have more than one plan up her skirt."

"Can we shadow them with a high-altitude drone and get some good intel on the second signature?"

"I think so. I'll call Pak and see what he can do. The bloke will lose his mind after we tell him we scuttled the ship."

"I'm tired of his shit. Put up or shut up. You want this, it takes resources, right Augustus?"

“Fuck yeah. Tell the Chinaman to get with it.” was his reply.

“Skipper, we close enough to launch?”

“Yes, sir.”

“How long will it take us to close on the sub after it’s disabled?”

“About ten minutes after we launch, we should be at their location.”

“Launch the damn thing, then, and let’s see what happens. I hope you are right on the EMP pulse, as I don’t want any casualties or damage to the device. Let it go George.”

“Roger that, one away and counting. Time to intercept around three minutes.” George beamed as he hit the launch button.

He just loves blowin' shit up. In three minutes, the world is going to change in our favor. It will be nice to get the upper hand for once. This time, I win.

“Holy crap, this guy is a real striker. I think the punk just launched something at us. Three minutes to intercept.” Josh yelled as Mum grabbed the ship’s mike.

"All hands prepare to abandon ship. Make yer way to the pods and get in, strap yerself in for immediate launch. Josh, Maria, and Thumper get in the pod. I'll be there on the quick." Mum announced with her usual sense of calm.

The three crewmen were in and gone as we made our way to the last pod. The fact that we were a bit on the slow side saved our lives.

"Thirty seconds to impact." I yelled "Let's get the hell out of this bloody coffin."

"Okay, let's do it, Thumper." Josh yelled, scrambling to the pod.

As we made our way forward, we could hear the missile approaching underwater. Suddenly it was silent, as if it had stopped. The concussion was enormous, and the sub rocked almost ninety degrees in the water. All electronics went out immediately. Maria was thrown against the bulkhead and received a nasty gash on her arm, knocking her unconscious. Mum was slammed to the floor and knocked out.

The sub was slowly trying to right itself and debris was everywhere. Alarms were blaring and I could hear the sub hull creaking and groaning.

Mum's left leg slammed into some equipment and fractured both the upper and lower part of her leg. On the upper part we could see bone sticking out, and she was bleeding badly. Josh had just made it to the pod and strapped in. He immediately unstrapped and turned back to help Mum and Maria.

I was thrown halfway across the deck but picked myself up, dusted off some imaginary dirt and yelled. "Bloody damn bugger. I will kill the bloke when I see him. Josh, grab Maria and get her in the pod. I got Mum. We need to get underway."

"Ya got it, mate. That bloody hurt like hell. What the hell was it?" Josh asked as he sat Maria in a seat and strapped her in.

"Not too damn sure. The bugger had an EMP pulse in it though; fried all the electronics. We will have to mechanically eject the pod from the sub. No time to scuttle her, we will have to just get the hell out." I muttered as I gingerly put Mum in a seat and strapped her in.

"Hey mate, give a look on Mum's leg and see if ye can stop the bleeding." I instructed.

"On it, Thumper. Let's get the hell out of here."

When the pod exited the sub, we saw what was left of the other escape pod through the small porthole in the forward section. All three men were dead, and the pod torn to pieces from the concussion. If we'd popped out with them, we'd have met a similar fate. As we floated to the surface, a pressure activated beacon launched and initiated a homing beacon. I just hoped the Royals got here before DM. As we hit the surface I saw a bloody fine sight, a Sikorsky hovering over us with a hook descending rapidly. About a click away I could see a sub buster flying above the surface looking for our attacker. Hope they found the bugger and jacked him up, I thought.

"You got it Thumper? Need any help?" Josh asked.

"No worries, mate, I'm all over it. Just take care of Mum. I replied and attached the hook to the pod when it descended.

As we landed on the fantail of the destroyer, the medics hit the pod, got Mum and Maria on gurneys and headed to the infirmary. We knew they would be okay, as Mum is tuff and has seen her share of knocks and Maria is cut from the same cloth. All I wanted was a chance to knock DM in the dirt for some serious payback.

Chapter 20 – Deception

"Fuck, fuck, fuck!! They were the fucking decoy. Holy shit we are in for it now. Dive this pig and put us on the bottom before the friggin' Royal Navy finds us and sends a missile up our ass." I screamed in frustration.

"Roger, Sam. Want me to send a sit-rep to Yong Pak?" Augustus asked.

My head was buzzing, thinking of all the ramifications of my actions. All we could hope for now is that he will hang with us and let us try to redeem ourselves. But shit, I sunk a destroyer of his with twenty men onboard. Got the Royal Navy barkin' up our ass and still no sign of Potts or Catherine.

"Augustus, get Pak on a secure line. Give him course and speed on the last known position of the other magma disturbance. He should have the drones up by now." I scowled. "We're screwed. We will be lucky if Pak doesn't try to take us out and we won't see a penny. The dicks above don't know if we are friendly or not, so we should be okay. Set a new course for the North Sea and push this sub as hard as it will go. If I didn't think they would find us I would send a torpedo into Catherine's freakin' sub and blow it all to hell." I commanded.

"Roger that, Sam. I hope you know what the bloody hell you're doing. Pak is going to be pissed mate. Lost the bloody bitch and sank one of his toys. Bad day to be you, mate." Augustus shook his head as he sat at the communications console.

"Just fuckin' do it. I'll take care of Pak." I grumbled.

"All right let's get on the surface and make the dash for Aberdeen." said Catherine.

"You got it, Cat." was Tim's reply. "Todd, level off at five meters and let's see who is about before we pop out."

"Roger that, Tim." I sat anxiously waiting for news of our friends.

"Michelle, what do you have on the sat link and radar?" Tim asked.

"It is very bad, mon ami. Mum is not on the sub. It looks like the three of the crew members are dead. The men are cowards, these DM. I will show them the edge of a sharp blade and make a new smile for them, non?" Michelle said with a look of total malice.

"Sit rep, on the subs last known position. I want confirmation from the Royals as to their safety and condition. Now!" commanded Catherine.

"They are on the Royal Navy destroyer Henry. The sub is not sunk, but dead in the water. Josh and Thumper have bumps and bruises but are okay. Mum has a broken leg and Maria has a concussion. They are being treated. The Royals will tow the sub in later. She is on the surface and floating. No hull damage, but Thumper said all the electronics are fried, including the H-Drive. He wants to know what they are to do next." Michelle said with a sense of relief.

"Tell my giant friend thank you, and I will send instructions within the hour. Thank you, Michelle and apologies for being short."

"Oui, madam, it is all as it should be. I worry about Mum, also."

"Tim, put us on top. Michelle, contact the US Navy and let us get to Aberdeen as soon as we can."

"You got it skipper. Headed for the surface and pushing this sub to maximum speed. I want out of these shark infested waters." Tim chuckled nervously, "Hey Cat, something weird is approaching us fast. Not sure what it is." Then he yelled "Brace yourself; impact imminent."

And those were the last words I heard.

Chapter 21 – Something

"Mr. Pak, the drones are away. They are on an intercept course with the last known position of their sub." Julius said.

"Fine, and the condition of our destroyer, please." I asked.

"Sir, the ship is gone. There are eleven survivors out of twenty men. The captain is in critical condition and the rest are injured but stable."

"Does anyone remember me giving permission for anyone to destroy my ship and crew?"

"No sir" was the nervous reply from all who sat at stations in the com bunker with Yong Pak.

"One certainly hopes that Mr. Craze had a very good reason for his actions. Now it appears the Royal Navy has them under surveillance, and they are considered combatants or terrorists. I am not sure which. I am not pleased with the current state of affairs, and Mr. Craze has some serious explaining to do."

"Yes sir." all replied in chorus.

"Have we identified the small signature of the other vehicle yet?"

"No sir, but we are doing high altitude fly overs. We have three drones in the air, sir. Two of them are armed and the other is recon only. I believe the U.S. has picked them up on radar and sent two jets up to investigate. What are your instructions, sir?" Julius asked me.

"In a moment." I replied as I sat, thinking quickly.

Sam has really caused me great expense and consternation. I will deal with him later. Right now, I must decide the fate of my dear friend, William, and his invention. I cannot allow him to share it with the world. It will create an imbalance that man is not prepared for. It must be used to enhance society and the endeavors of the very brightest human beings. I believe William's very naive view of man will encourage him into sharing his new technology with the world. We are not prepared for that. Perhaps I can with a little luck and some diligence repeat his performance soon. Apologies, my old friend, but I must act.

"Julius, what is the status of our drones?"

"We have found the other submersible, sir. It appears to be a flying wing of sorts and moving very fast on the surface. The U.S. Navy is closing on their position in an escort deployment."

"Engage the target and destroy it. I want no survivors. Am I clear?"

"Yes sir. But will we not destroy the device also?"

"Yes, and my dear friend William will also perish. Do as I command!" I barked with only the slightest feeling of remorse.

"Attack formation Delta 3. Run the recon drone in first and target the device. Spread formation on the other two drones and target the con area of the ship." Julius instructed the other two drone pilots.

"Aye." they replied as I watched the screens. The drones carried two sub busters each, which would be more than enough for a craft of this size. The only thing that could stop them now was the escorts or the two Raptors that were fast approaching. The timing would be close, but I knew that I had the edge.

"Two minutes to target, sir."

"Mankind will thank me one day for my efforts." I mused. William would be a loss, so brilliant, but incredibly naïve.

Chapter 22 – Disaster

"Bridge, radar over" said the chief from the radar room aboard the USS Ronald Reagan A nuclear class aircraft carrier.

"Go ahead radar." Commander Trowel responded.

"We have three drones on intercept course with the vessel we are to escort." replied the chief.

"Do we have jets in the air?" said Trowel.

"Roger that, sir."

"Consider the drones hostile and take all offensive efforts to debilitate or destroy them. Am I clear?" Commander James Trowel, the captain of the Ronald Reagan commanded.

"Aye aye, sir. Attention, wing commander and planes aloft. Engage targets at your earliest and destroy with extreme prejudice. Do you copy?"

"Copy that." the wing commander said.

"Roger that." was the almost simultaneous reply from the two Raptors in the air.

"Target 1 acquired and sidewinders away."

"Target two acquired and sidewinders away."

"Closing on third target. Thirty seconds to radar lock and we will splash all three."

"Unable to lock on third target. Evasive maneuvers are too erratic. Switching to guns. Over."

"Roger that. Do it quickly captain, we are out of time." said Trowel.

"I have gun lock and am firing at the last drone. Drone is hit but has launched its missiles. They have acquired the target. Sorry skipper, just a hair late. The sub has been hit, sir."

"Roger that, Captain. Stay in the air and run a sweep of the area. We'll put two more Raptors up."

"Aye, Aye, sir."

"Jim, put two rescue choppers in the air and get to their last position. Alert sick bay causalities on the way. All ships defense pattern Charlie six. This is not a drill. I repeat this is not a drill."

"Skipper, rescue Zulu One here. Divers in the water. Craft is dead in the water. No apparent hull breach, but no response to our attempts to contact the occupants. She's sealed up tight skipper, and we are not sure how to get inside."

"Roger that, Zulu One. Stay with the craft. Jim, do we have anything big enough to lift them out of the water?" Trowel asked with concern and urgency.

"Maybe Skipper, give me one minute. said Jim. "Skipper, the sky crane is fueled and ready to launch."

"Thanks Jim, get that beast in the air and let's get that craft on the flight deck asap! We need to get inside quickly and assess the occupants' condition. Move, people!"

For Captain Trowell it felt like an eternity but was only about four minutes before they were lowering the sub-plane onto the deck. The wings were partly retracted and misshapen, obviously from the two direct hits it had sustained. He could see the impact sights, but almost no indentations and not a sign of a hull breach.

"Skipper, Tim here, rescue one. We found the hatch, sir, and will be inside in a moment."

"Roger that, Tim. Get the med techs next to the craft and ready to go."

"Aye aye, sir. We're in, skipper, and it's not good. Three are pretty banged up. One dead and one is pretty shaken up but looks to be in one piece. Heading to the

Med station now and will get the surgeon to call you with an update."

"Good work, Tim, and let me know as soon as you can."

"Skipper, con. The president is on the line, sir. In your stateroom or on the bridge, sir?"

"I'll take call in my room. Thanks, Pete." Commander Trowel replied, wondering what was so important that the President was calling.

Chapter 23 – Death

In sick bay, it was chaotic, with Doctors and corpsmen attending to the injured. Organized chaos was a good way to describe their efforts and movements.

"Corpsman, give that man a sedative. What's your name, mister?"

"Potts, my name is William Potts. What happened to us?" I was dazed.

"As far as we can tell you got nailed by two "Sub Busters" and were damn lucky to survive. How do I get these damn suits off these people? They need treatment immediately if we are to save their lives." said Commander Rakes, the onboard surgeon.

"Uh, uh, I'm not sure." I muttered.

"Commander, the vital signs of this one is approaching very low levels."

"Potts, if you can help, great, if not, get your ass out of here."

"Yes, yes. I remember. In the ship is a small red case and a silver one slightly larger. I need them both immediately, and we can remove the Suits. Hurry." I shook my head.

Soon I had the cases and opened them. In about two minutes I had set them up and typed furiously into a keyboard. I watched as with a final keystroke, Todd's suit left his body and hung in a corner of the room. Then Catherine's, then Tim's. Michelle was not in the room. The team of doctors began to work furiously on all three at the same time. It seemed like forever, but only about an hour passed before they were all stable. All were unconscious, but breathing easy, and their vital signs appeared stable.

"Commander, where is Michelle?" I asked anxiously.

"I'm sorry, sir, she didn't make it. She was dead when we finally got in the ship." Mr. Rakes replied.

"What! Dead? No, she can't be. I must check at once and see if she can be revived. Where is she?" I demanded.

"She's in the morgue, and the damage to her is irreparable, I'm afraid. Severe facial trauma and both lungs completely collapsed. I'm sorry, sir. You may see her if you like."

"No, no, I understand. It's just such a shock. She was so full of life just moments ago." I felt the tears form and slide down my cheeks.

"Would you like to see the Chaplain, sir?"

"No, I'll be fine. May I stay with my friends?"

"I believe the captain would like to see you on the bridge sir."

"Okay, I will do what I can. Will someone show me the way?" I asked. They were all trying to help me, and people were dead or injured. This may be a debt I can never repay, I sorrowfully thought.

"Yes sir, and if you begin to feel nauseous or faint, take one of these. If you experience unmanageable pain, take one of these." He handed me two pill bottles. "If you experience any blurred vision or black dots in your field of vision, report to me or let a corpsman know right away. You have sustained a mild concussion and have some bruising that these meds should help. Am I clear, sir?" The commander asked.

"Yes and thank you. I will do as you say. I believe I am ready to see the captain now." I replied.

As we walked through the ship my mind raced. Michelle dead and the other three so badly injured. I wonder who hated me so. I had no enemies that I knew of. After what seemed like an eternity of stairs and passages, we came to what I assumed was the bridge. It looked very military and there were many men giving and receiving orders in a beautiful ballet of efficiency. The captain was a striking man with an air of assurance about him, much like Catherine. Dressed in Navy combat fatigues he looked to be in his fifties with the sides of his hair beginning to grey. He looked very fit and seemed to be in total command of the ship and the situation.

"Mr. Potts? May I call you William?" Captain Trowel asked.

"Yes, certainly, sir. How can I be of help?" Potts responded.

"For starters, let me welcome you to the Ronald Reagan and I can assure you, the safety of you and your fellow crewman is my priority. Is there anything you need before we head to the United States?" asked Captain Trowel.

"Yes, we must secure the craft we were in. There is a device inside in a protective case that needs to be secured and out of sight. I would like to inspect it before we store it, if possible." I insisted nervously.

"Absolutely. Pete, get an armed escort. Take Potts to the craft. After he has inspected his device, I want it secured in the ship weapons locker and a twenty-four-hour guard placed around the device. Am I clear?"

"Aye aye, sir. If you will follow me, Mr. Potts." Pete responded.

Upon entering the aerosub, I went straight to the pod that FEAT was in. Opening the case and running a quick diagnostic check I found everything exactly as it should be. Not a hint of damage and in perfect working order. I stayed with them until it was in the safety of the weapons locker and then asked to be returned to the bridge.

"Captain, do you have any idea who attacked us?" I inquired.

"Well, we know it was a group that calls themselves DM and that a man by the name of Yong Pak leads them." the captain said angrily.

"What! Yong Pak. He was my lab mate at MIT and my very best friend. We parted company but I cannot believe he would try to kill me." I said incredulously.

"I'm afraid so, Mr. Potts. Our intel is very accurate, and we are currently along with England, Denmark and a few other countries attempting to find him." said Commander Trowel.

"I find that very hard to believe, captain, and I hope you are wrong. We must get to the secure sight in Wyoming as soon as we are able that I might set up the device and take care of my injured companions. How long will it take to get to the U.S., and may I go below and check on my friends?"

"Of course, you can. There is a jet transport being fueled as we speak. A team of doctors and aides will go with you. A fighter escort will take you to a secure strip in the Wyoming mountains and from there to a secure bunker. Our orders are very clear. Get you, your team and the device to Wyoming at all costs. Your friends are being loaded onto the plane as we speak, and I wish you Godspeed sir. I'm not sure what your device does but everyone is excited about your safety. Good luck to you and your team. I hope you all recover quickly." the captain said as he extended his hand.

"Thank you for all you have done." I said, leaving for the flight deck.

Chapter 24 – Asylum

"Todd can you hear me? Todd, wake up. Can you hear me?" Slowly, I regained consciousness. Where was that voice coming from? Am I dreaming? I want to wake up. Who is calling my name? Why can't I wake up? Am I dead? I wondered groggily.

The voice spoke again. "Todd don't fight. You have a tube in your throat helping you breathe. You have been injured, and we are trying to help you. If you understand nod your head." I heard the anxiety as I recognized Williams' voice.

I could understand him but felt like I was in a dark fog with no sense of direction. Something was in my throat, and I wanted it out. Stay calm, I told myself. There must be a reason. It was all slowly coming back to me. The ship, an explosion, then darkness. I nodded my head yes in response to the question.

"Todd, I wish to use FEAT on you. You have been severely injured, and I don't think the doctors can help you completely. There is some damage to your back that their skills will not be able to repair. I know that the device will fix it and make you as you were. Do I have your permission?" asked Potts.

I nodded my head in the affirmative as I drifted back into the darkness.

I tried to open my eyes, but the light hurt. Then, I heard a voice. "Todd, cough for me, please. We are going to remove your breathing tube. Easy now, just relax, it will be over in a minute." the deep, soothing voice instructed.

I felt as if a garden hose was stuffed down my throat. I could feel it leaving as I coughed. It was not pleasant at all, and as soon as it cleared my mouth, I gasped for air. A mask was placed over my mouth and nose, and that helped quite a bit. I could breathe, but my throat was sore. I tried to talk but all that came out was a little squeak.

"You're fine, son. Don't try to talk just yet. Let the swelling go down, and in an hour or two you should be able to speak. If you have any pain, nod once for yes and twice for no. You have been through a lot but are doing remarkably well. William's device is extraordinary. I have never witnessed anyone healing at the rate you are. Truly amazing." said someone.

What? Potts had used the device on me? I did feel different. My back hurt some, but other than that I felt pretty good. I nodded my head twice, opening my eyes. Lifting my arm, I made an eating motion. This amused everyone in the room. And where was everyone? I didn't recognize any of these people, but they sure seemed glad to see me awake.

"In a couple of hours, Todd, I can get you some food. We need the swelling in your throat to go down a little more before you try to swallow more than air. Do you understand?"

Nodding my head once, I tried to take stock of my surroundings. I had no clue where we were but could only guess on land somewhere as there was no rocking motion. I was in a bed in a normal-looking hospital room. I tried to remember what happened. Then I remembered. The incoming rockets on the radar and a huge explosion. I felt like I was flying for a moment, then felt a sharp stabbing pain in my back, then nothing.

Sure would like to see everyone, I thought as I began to drift back into sleep. My thoughts rambled, hope Michelle and Catherine are okay, wonder if Tim got banged up. He was right beside me. Potts was in the back strapped in. Hope he is okay. I'm tired; hopefully I will get some chow soon. Starvin'.

"I have to tell you, Mr. Potts, your device is the most brilliant thing I've ever witnessed." the Chief of Surgery said with a look of amazement. "If you had told me you could repair the damage to those three human beings by changing the frequency of their atoms and DNA, I would have called you a quack. I have never seen anything like it. I would love to have a discussion sometime about how you designed and researched your invention to completion. Mr. Peters' back was broken in three places. I have no clue what kept him alive until you helped him, except perhaps strength of will. And the other two cases were just as impressive. Catherine's injuries were most grievous, and Tim was in bad shape. It would appear they will make a full recovery, thanks to you." said Commander Rakes, Chief of Surgery. He looked military but not the stiff soldier kind. Tall, maybe six foot four and in good shape. A little on the young side for a Chief of Surgery, he looked to be in his mid-30s.

"Thank you, sir. I am just a simple tinkerer with a good idea. A lot of it was an accident but I did have a good idea once or twice." I responded modestly.

"You are much too modest. The entire facility is buzzing with the possibilities. We hear the President, and his cabinet will be here in two days to talk with you. Are you ready for that?" asked Rakes.

"No, I am not. The reality of what FEAT can do is setting in, and I now know the morality of the device is perhaps more than I was prepared for. Does that make sense?"

"Yes, it does. Mankind has been plagued throughout history with devices intended to free him from pain or physical burden. Each time there seems to be a group or country with a totally different agenda. Interesting problem men such as you face. I have brought a few men back from the gates of death and had wished afterwards that I had let them die. Evil is aberrant to me, and those men were the epitome of evil. So, I know now how you must feel." Rakes said in a somber tone.

"Yes, my position has changed a bit after the events of the last few days and weeks. I'm not sure this should be for everyone. How do we choose? It is a problem. Evil must not be allowed to flourish, and I'm afraid my discovery would create a societal group of malcontents and cause more damage to man. I need good counsel for sure." I said, as I rubbed my chin thoughtfully.

"Well, let's get some rest sir. Tomorrow is a big day. All your friends will be close to a full recovery if they stay at the present rate of healing. I'm still blown away by the speed at which they are recovering." Rakes said earnestly.

"Good night, Commander, and thank you for your help with my friends and the conversation. It means a lot to me."

And with that we parted and headed to our quarters. He was right, though, that tomorrow would be a huge day for everyone. I hoped everyone could deal with the loss of Michelle. It had been hard for me to experience her loss without being able to talk to any of my friends.

Chapter 25 – Safety

I felt good. I had not felt like this since my mid-twenties. I wanted to go see everybody. I thought, I'll just get up and go see them. As I swung my legs over the bed, I felt a sharp twinge in several places along my back.

"Whoa there, Mr. Peters, not so fast. Let me help you. Here get in this wheelchair, and I'll take you wherever you want to go." said the nurse, a pleasant looking young man with a nice smile. He looked capable.

"Okay. My back is kinda' sore. What happened to me?" I asked in a pained expression.

"I'm not supposed to say, but you broke your back in three places. But you are healing fast. The docs can't believe it. Would have killed anyone else. That machine sure fixed you up." The nurse said with a note of awe.

"Thanks, I won't tell anyone. Can I get some chow, and then I would like to see my team." I asked eagerly.

"Sure, let's go. The food here is great."

I was not quite sure where we were, but if I had to guess from Catherines' conversations we were at the hardened facility in Wyoming. It was a marvel of technology. Everything was crisp and clean, with voice activated monitors everywhere. The lighting made it seem as if we were outside, even though I suspected we were deep inside a mountain.

"Pretty cool, huh. We bring the air in, filter it and run it through our scrubbers. This protects our air supply from outside tampering. Then we scent it with different smells for different sections: forest, ocean, and plains, to name a few. The lighting was created to feel and look like sunlight. We have an atrium where you can experience everything from snow to desert heat." the nurse revealed.

"What's your name?" I asked.

"Most people call me John. My first name is Tiberius. I like John better. Sounds like Greek otherwise." he chuckled.

"Well, Tiberius, let us make to the mess hall in our trusty chariot."

That brought a laugh from him. I felt amazing, ready for anything. Potts' device really works, and I was enjoying the new me.

“Blue x-ray 7, mess hall access please.” John spoke as we approached a set of doors.

The doors silently slid into the wall, and what looked like a four-star restaurant was spread out before us.

“Wow! You guys sure know how to live.” I said in wonder.

“I think Catherine and Tim are at a table already. I will put you with them, and someone will be by to take your order.” John wheeled me to their table.

“Thanks, John, that would be great.”

As we drew close to their table, I could see Tim had his head hung low and Catherine had her head in her hands, softly crying.

“Hey guys, how is it going? Why is everyone so sad?” I asked.

Catherine stood and moved towards me slowly. She appeared to be having trouble walking but was by my side in a moment. I could see that her face was moist from crying.

“Todd, I have some bad news. We just found out that Michelle didn’t make it.” Catherine said, bleary eyed.

I suddenly felt sick to my stomach, and the urge to scream was overwhelming. I could hardly believe it. My sweet Michelle. I had grown very fond of her and thought she would always be in my life. I was stunned and instinctively reached for Catherine and pulled her as close as the chair would allow. Her gentle sobs touched me to the depths of my soul. I had not felt this kind of loss in a very long time.

“Cat, I don’t know what to say. I’m stunned. Are you ok? Tim, are you okay? How is Potts doing?

“Yeah, I’m fine, brother, just hurtin'. Loved that girl more than she probably knew. She was special to the team, and she will be missed.” Tim replied.

“I’m better now, knowing that you will recover from your injuries my love. Michelle’s passing is a great loss.” Catherine said.

We all picked at our food, managing to get a few bites down. We tried to exchange small talk but found it hard to continue our conversation. Potts strolled up to us and asked to sit down.

"May I join you?"

"Yes." was our chorus.

"I was hoping to give you the news about Michelle. I went and saw her after we arrived here. She was severely injured. Massive cranial damage. She never felt a thing. I could not have saved her even with FEAT. I will miss that sweet child. So full of life and always a cheerful word or a hug for everyone." William said in a comforting tone. "The device has done amazing things for all of you. Todd, you were the most severely injured. Your back was broken in three places and there was major swelling of your spinal cord. You had seven broken ribs, and your right lung was punctured and collapsed. Catherine, you had two broken legs and a severe closed head wound. The blood clot was sizable, but we were able to stabilize you until we could get you here and use the device on you. And my dear Tim. It appeared you broke everything. Both legs, one arm and half a dozen ribs. There were lacerations to your right flank and a ruptured spleen. I believe if we had not modified the Suits, none of us would have made it."

He continued, "I believe that we should honor Michelle's memory and move forward. She would have wanted us to celebrate her life and not mourn her death. The news is sudden, but in a day or two you will begin to see my point. Lift your glasses, please. To our dear, sweet Michelle LeFont. May God hold her in his bosom and may we honor her memory by fulfilling our goals and the team's goals." William smiled softly as he spoke.

He was right. We should honor her life and not dwell on her passing. We would miss her, and all of us would have time to grieve in our own way.

"Of course, my dear William, you are right. We shall honor her memory. I would like to see everyone in my room. May we go now?" Catherine asked as she struggled with the news.

"Yes." we all replied somberly.

As our somber quartet made its way through the boulevards, we were all deep in thought. How fleeting is the thing called life. With all our technology we really were only one breath away from death A sobering thought, and I would miss her immensely. My time with her was special, and I will never forget her smile or her playful nature.

As we approached Catherine's room, we all were getting over the initial shock. When we entered, she motioned for us all to not speak for a moment. Nodding to William he took what could have passed for a Blackberry out of his coat pocket. Typing in a few numbers he gave the all clear.

"What is all this about, Catherine?" I asked.

"We have a big problem. The man that I had been speaking to regarding our safety and the protection of the device has mysteriously been, how should I say, misplaced. William and I believe that the device is either going to be stolen from us or they will attempt to keep us here against our will. We must play this close to the chest and go along with them. The team from England will be here this afternoon. Mum, Maria, Josh and Thumper are a big part of my plan to get us out of this mess. I don't know how I was so easily deceived. I thought surely the U.S. could be trusted. And perhaps they could, but the present administration has no honor and must have reevaluated their agenda after learning what FEAT can do. We do have an ace in the hole. The four of us here have all been subjected to the benefits of FEAT. William, if you will explain please." Catherine said with just a hint of anger among all the emotions we had going on.

William looked at each one of us slowly with that funky Einsteinian look he had.

"The President and his cabinet will be here tomorrow. Nine of them want to experience the benefits of the device. I have been able to fine tune the results so that it will appear that they have reaped the benefits that we have. However, the effects will have a short life span of perhaps a month. Our intention is to escape this place and make it to a secure sight in Canada. Vancouver to be exact. Am I right, Catherine?"

"Yes, William, continue."

"Our plan is to establish a group of people we will call RISK. Responsible Individuals Seeking Knowledge. Our original intention was to make the device available to the world. After careful consideration Catherine and I think that man collectively is not ready for this technology. Our intention now is to apply the benefits of the device to people we think will enhance mankind's journey. A panel will be established to help make the decisions." William explained.

"William, isn't that kind of like playing God?" I asked.

"My dear Todd, I hope not. But short of destroying the device and all the benefits it will create I'm not sure what to do. I hope we will be good stewards of this gift and use it for man's enhancement, and not his demise." William said somberly.

"William and I have spoken at length about this even while we were in England. We had hoped that the U.S. would have been good partners, but we were sadly wrong. We can either destroy it and hope it comes along when man is prepared, or we can take our chances and attempt to save man from himself. We believe the latter to be in the planet's best interest. Tomorrow morning, we will reveal the plan to get out of here. It won't be easy, as you can see how difficult it is to move around in the facility, let alone actually breach the defenses of this place and get inside. Everything is voice activated, and there is surveillance everywhere. The timing must be perfect. With that said, no more talk until tomorrow. William, turn off the audio playback diffuser and lets all have a conversation as it relates to our latest experiences." Catherine instructed in a somber tone.

Chapter 26 – Accountability

“Well, Mr. Craze, what kind of excuse do you wish to present this time?” Yong Pak angrily asked me.

“I don’t have one Mr. Pak. They clearly got the best of me and my team. I offer my apologies for the loss of the ship and the lives involved. At the moment, it seemed like the right thing to do. Did the drones have any success?” I replied coldly.

“No, Mr. Craze we were only partially successful. The U.S. Navy intercepted our efforts before we could close on their position. The drones did have the desired effect of at least rendering their craft inoperable. The fact that we could not secure Potts or the device is unfortunate. We know they are in a hardened facility in Wyoming and will be very hard to extract. However, we have it under good authority that the U.S. is not going to honor their commitment to Catherine, Potts and her group. We may be able to yet convince Mr. Potts of the folly of his ways and get him to see our way of thinking.” Pak said menacingly.

"Well, sir, I have no idea how you will be able to do that. The facility they are at is very secure and has the resources of the entire country at their disposal." I said.

"I agree, Mr. Craze. However, there is always a way. I believe we have found a way to cause an evacuation of the facility, and that will be our opportunity to secure or terminate Potts and the device. Your recent attempts have been a dismal failure. However, I will extend one more opportunity to you and your team. If you fail this time, I will see to it that your name will not fall easily on anyone's ears. Do I have your attention?" Pak said without an ounce of emotion.

I held my anger in thinking that maybe I should just whack him first. It might be safer in the long run. Screw the money, always another client out there. But now is not the right time. Have patience!

"All right, Pak. I hate having a mission end so badly. I will stick it out for just a bit longer. Now, what is your plan?"

"We have found their fresh air intakes and know how to incapacitate their scrubbers. We will introduce a low-level biological agent to their air supply, which will render them unconscious. We have most of the access codes to the facility and believe we can get the rest once inside. The facility has enormous safety protocols in place, and it will be hard to overcome physically. But perhaps with a little stealth and some modern bio tech we can complete our mission yet." he said with just a hint of pride.

"Okay, sounds feasible. Lay it out for me."

Chapter 27 – Reunited

The reunion that afternoon was bittersweet. Potts had used the device on everyone but Thumper. He was not interested in immortality just yet. After a couple of hours, we all convened in the mess hall. Everyone was somber for a few moments as we digested the loss of Michelle. But soon we spoke of successes and near misses and found joy that most of us had made it. Mum's broken legs were healing nicely. Maria was not badly injured, just knocked out and some bumps and bruises. FEAT had taken care of most of their injuries and William said the cast on Mum's leg could probably be removed by the end of the day. We ate some food, drank a little wine and shared the experiences of the last week.

"How is the retreat on the English northern coast, Mum?" Catherine asked.

"It will tidy up nicely. The men will have it in good nick in a fortnight or less. Most of the damage was in the garage area. We found one poor bloke encased in the foam. Not a lovely way to go to be sure." Mum responded.

"How about the facility outside of Denmark, Maria?" Catherine continued.

"It looks good—hardly any damage at all. Some light damage to the doors, but an easy fix." Maria responded.

"Good, I'm glad to hear that. After we finish eating let's all retire to my room for a cocktail." Catherine suggested expectantly.

Everyone nodded in agreement.

When we were close to Catherine's room two men stopped us. "Mr. Potts the president wishes to see a demonstration of the device in the morning. Will you be prepared sir?" the Colonel asked.

"Yes sir, in the morning will be fine. What time will he arrive, and who is the subject?" William asked.

"Be ready at ten, and it will be the Vice President and then the President." the Colonel replied.

"As you wish. Until morning then." Potts responded with a slight grin.

Upon entering Catherine's room, William produced his Blackberry and repeated the performance of the other day.

"Are we good, William?" she asked.

"Yes, we are fine, we can speak freely. We will have about ten minutes before the signal begins to degrade and their safety sweeps change frequencies." William explained.

Everyone was intent on hearing the plan. We were rested and on the mend. It was nice to see everyone so focused. Each of us found a place to sit and we collectively turned our attention to Catherine.

"Okay, let's get to it. Save your questions until I've finished; we don't have much time. Some of what I'm about to tell you will seem preposterous but bear with me until I've finished. In the morning about nine thirty, just as the President arrives, all hell will break loose. As hard as this is to believe, DM is going to play a big part in our escape. I know it seems impossible; however, it's true. We know they are going to make another attempt to kidnap William and steal the device." She clearly had us on the edge of our seats listening to every word. You could see the determination and trust in each of our faces.

"We have a man on the inside of DM who has been helping us for a while now. I have secured a transmission device that escapes all detection and broadcasts on such a low frequency that it is almost unrecognizable. With this device I have been in contact with our inside man. This is one of the reasons we have been able to stay one step ahead of DM. We know that DM has figured out a way to introduce a chemical agent into the fresh air intakes. He will also render the air scrubbers useless, and the facility will suffer the full impact of the chemical agent. We believe it to be a nerve agent that will render the victim unconscious for several hours. William has assured us that we are not vulnerable to much of anything as our cells repair or assimilate any foreign object almost immediately. Thumper, you, however, will not be immune. We have fashioned a respirator that should protect you. We also think Yong Pak has the codes to all the exit ports. We have a few, and William has assured me when the time comes, we will have the rest. Getting out of the facility will be hard but not impossible with Pak's unintentional help. Getting to Canada will be the hard part." she continued. Everyone looked at her anxiously as she unfolded her plan.

"As soon as the facility detects an intrusion of any kind, it sends out an automatic alert to all the combined Armed Forces of the U.S. We will have about eleven minutes before this place will be blanketed with air, ground and satellite surveillance and support. Yong knows this also and will strike at precisely the right moment. We believe he will have a couple of attack helicopters and two Sikorsky troop carriers armed to the teeth. This will be the perfect distraction. While he scrambles to find us, we will let him find the device, except for NAT. Without NAT and the frequencies, the device is useless. We think he will be so happy to put his hands on it that he won't notice the missing parts. We are sure he will make a frontal assault and come straight in, and we plan to set up just inside the doors for the President and his staff. There is a small service tunnel just outside of this room that leads to a maintenance area. As soon as everyone is incapacitated, we will head there. William has put a holographic device in place, and it will show us unconscious like the rest. It won't fool anyone for very long, but we don't need much time. The satellite sweeps are very close together, and Pak knows this. He will be detected, but we think he has planned for this. After the alarm has sounded, the satellite will begin to track the area for intruders. There should be about a four-minute delay from the moment of detection until they have eyes on us. That should be just enough time. About half a click from here is an abandoned silver mine. No one has been in it for years. It is undetectable from the air, and short of knowing exactly where it is you would never know it was there." she said intently.

"We have about four minutes to make it from here to there. All of us are healing but none of us are to full capacity yet. We must make it! If we don't, it's over. We will be assassinated, and the device stolen. There are supplies in the mine and the shaft goes on for quite a while. We know that it connects to a series of caves through the Wyoming mountain range. We started preparing our escape route the moment we made our plans with the U.S." Catherine said somberly.

Each of us in turn looked at each other and then back to Catherine. Our mutual respect was obvious to all of us as we listened intently to her plan.

"One can never be too prepared, as we have found out. With some careful planning and some good luck, we will be in Canada in about a week. It will take about three days of walking and climbing in the caves to get to a safe exit point. When we exit the cave deep in the mountains, we will have a four-day trek on foot in the thick forest of a Wyoming valley. We will all put on our suits tonight and cover them with regular clothing. Once outside the facility we will discard the clothing as it will create a thermal signature. William has modified the Suit even further so that it will render any thermal sweeps useless. This will be important when we exit the caves, as there will be sweeps of the area in an ever-widening circle. Once outside and in the open we will travel at night. We must travel about twenty-five miles at night in rough terrain to get to the extraction point. When we get there our people from Vancouver will be waiting to help us get to perhaps our most secure site. There we will plan and decide what to do next. When you go to sleep tonight, wear the Suit. William has linked Nimmrod with their computer system. Just put the suit on, go to sleep, and in the morning, you will have all the details about our route through the caves and our final destination. We believe most of us who were hurt badly will be at about 75 percent by the morning. Todd and Tim will be the ones most likely to not be 100 percent. I know you all have a million questions. There is no time to answer them. When William turns off the device let us continue our conversations as if there was no interruption. Please refrain from any conversation amongst you until it all happens. It's unfortunate we were unable to trust our new allies. We will be the stewards of this new era, and with each other's help we will help usher in a new age of man. Good luck, and let's all get a glass and toast our success. Timing is crucial, and we will need to be spot on in the morning. William, disengage the device." she said as we all raised our glasses.

"As you wish Catherine, and good luck to all of us. Each one of you has become as family to me and I know we are doing the right thing. Bon Chance!" William said as he raised his glass in a toast.

We sat and visited for another couple of hours. Doing our best to contain our excitement. The mood around here had started to shift the last couple of days. It had a darker feeling than it did when we first arrived. It was as if everyone was holding their breath waiting. We went to dinner and then to our rooms. I put my Suit on and climbed into bed, soon drifting off to sleep.

Chapter 28 – Penetration

As we approached the site, I detected no activity at all. Just as Pak had planned. The team on the ground had done its job well.

"Sam, get in, get Potts and the device and let's get out of here as quickly as possible. We have a short window to make this successful. Augustus has rendered the site and its personnel unconscious. Be quick, as I'm sure the combined might of this country is on its way." Pak instructed.

"You got it. Let's get on the ground and get going. George, you ready? The rest of you lock and load and let's get this done." I said.

"I'm ready. Let's do this." George eagerly replied.

I'll get this one right, I mused. And I hope I get a shot at Catherine and her team. I will put them down this time. As we approached the doors, no one was in sight. From the safety of the chopper, Pak electronically opened the doors. Eight of us hit the opening and entered the facility. We moved to where Pak assured us Potts and the team would be. As we entered the doors, we could see that everyone was unconscious. Catherine and her team were seated slumped over in the gallery, and Potts was sitting at a computer station. The device was in plain view.

"Secure the device, and let's get the hell out of here. We got about two minutes to be in the air and gone."

"I got it." George said. He grabbed the device as another man disconnected it from the computer. As they started to leave, I said, "Finally, I found you, and you are mine." And with that, I sent a spray of lead directly into Catherine and her team. As the weapon discharged, I looked in disbelief. The bullets went right through them! All I could see was a shimmer of light as the lead passed through the obvious holograph. Son of a bitch! I thought to myself. She's gotten my ass again. At least this time we got the device. That should make the psycho Pak happy. How in the hell did she always stay one step ahead of us?

We boarded the choppers and got the hell out of there. I couldn't help but think that we had a problem. It was not by chance that she is always one step ahead of us. Someone must be feeding her information, and I need to find out who that someone is.

“Mr. Craze.” Pak said, pulling me back to the moment.

“Yes, sir.”

“Did you see Potts, Catherine and her team?”

“Well, I saw a very clever holograph of them. I sprayed it with about forty rounds and all I saw was the shimmer of the holographic field being disrupted. They were not physically there.”

“I find this puzzling. The device was there, yet none of their team was?”

“That is correct, Mr. Pak. We did, however, secure the device and all the connections. Now, let’s get the hell out of here, sir!”

“Yes, yes, we must hurry. Let us leave this area and get to safety. I’m sure help is on the way.”

I would be glad to get away from this guy. It has not been a good mission.

Chapter 29 – Escape

Just as Catherine said, about nine thirty everyone around us started dropping like flies. Thumper barely got his makeshift respirator on in time. Potts activated the holograph, we made our way to the maintenance room, and in a moment, we were outside and moving fast. All the supplies and gear were waiting for us in the mine, so we had nothing to carry.

We heard the choppers closing in as we made our way along the wash towards the mine. In no time, without incident we were in front of two huge boulders. As Catherine walked between them, or I should say, squeezed between them, I agreed with her. Unless you knew exactly where this was, you would never find it. Once inside, we saw a pile of gear and a lone man apparently waiting for our arrival. Catherine walked directly to him and gave him a big hug as if she had known him all her life.

“Hello, Augustus, are you ok?” she asked.

“Crackin’ good, Catherine, and glad to be away from those crazy blokes.” he smiled.

"Thanks for helping with everything. Are we ready to go?"

"Yes, we are. I'm scot free and ready to get on with it. Everyone has a very similar kit, and we have a proper path out of this cave and on to Canada." he pointed to the packs.

"All right then. Everyone, grab your gear, change into scrambling boots, put your packs on, and let's get going. We have a long way to go and need to keep moving. We will have a chance later in the day to introduce Augustus to you and explain our relationship. Right now, we need to get gone." Catherine urged.

"Tim, you and Todd bring up the rear, and Augustus, you take point. Augustus, do you have the map?" she asked.

"I do. I've been able to get a GPS to work some in this environment. We'll use it as a check from time to time. Just a way to tidy up the map a bit."

"All right, we need to get on then. Let's get out of here. Everyone okay and ready to push off?"

We nodded our heads and were on our way.

It was surreal being in an old mine, and trying to escape the U.S., Pak, and anyone else that wanted to snag us. It felt as if we were part of an apocalyptic planet where everything had gone wrong, and we were the only ones left alive.

I wondered where Augustus played into all of this. He must have been an asset of Catherine's. He was certainly glad to see her, and their reunion was one of long familiarity. I looked forward to having a chat with him.

Walking through the mine was not too bad, but when it broke off into the caves, it was an entirely different story. Up, down, left, right, in, out, always wet. Either wading through water or it dripped down on us from overhead. Sleeping at night was the hardest with so many weird noises. The Suit kept us warm, thanks to Potts and all the modifications he had made to it. Augustus was not so lucky. He stayed wet and miserable, and you could tell he was ready to be outside. We ate MRE's for breakfast, lunch and dinner. They were surprisingly good, and I started to look forward to them. There was not a lot of conversation, as everyone had to concentrate on the path during the day, and we were beat down at night only wanting to sleep. Mid-morning of the third day we approached the exit from the caves.

As we sat in the cave's opening, the sun beat down through a section of the ceiling. We huddled in the pool of light. It felt good to be warmed by the sun, and not to have to use our headlamps. Knowing that we were almost halfway to safety was comforting.

"So, Augustus, how do you know Cat?" I asked, taking a seat beside him.

"I knew her husband Arthur." he said "We were mates at Oxford and later we climbed together. Known them both for a bit now. Mum trained, me and I've known the team for years."

"I had no idea. Must have been hard, being the inside guy at DM."

"Yes. We had to keep a proper secret about me so if one of you blokes got caught you would not spill the beans."

"Well, we thank you for all the help. We always were one step ahead of them and I just thought it was good planning."

"It was mate. But with a little help, it was easy to sort out."

I walked over to where Catherine was and sat down next to her. I put my arm around her shoulders and gave her a squeeze. She turned and looked at me and gave me a weary smile. She was tired. She had small bags under each eye and her worry lines were more pronounced. Her whole body felt ready to rest, as did mine.

We rested for the remainder of the day. A nearby small stream provided a much-needed rinsing. Cold as it was, we reveled in the clear water. That night we headed out on the second leg of our journey.

Augustus was good. He had a mountaineer's sense of direction. What would work for the team and what would just be too difficult. Fortunately, all of us were almost up to a hundred percent. Thumper suffered the most of all as he had chosen not to use FEAT and his energy was starting to get low. Augustus led us through the mountains without incident. We could hear choppers in the air night and day. He was a great point man and got us to go places and do things I never would have attempted.

It was hard to believe I'd only known Catherine and Tim for less than a year. Mum and her group, even shorter. I was not the same man that got up enough courage to approach a woman in a bar and take a chance. My life was irreversibly changed for the good. I couldn't explain how I fell in love with Catherine, or how I felt about all these people. I had never been exposed to people that were so brave, yet so unselfish, and to be a part of their small circle was more than I could ever have dreamed of. I was truly becoming the man I always thought I could be.

We reached the extraction point without incident at daybreak. It was a lake that served as an exit and entry point for naturalists and hunting groups. The floatplanes that were to pick us up had not arrived. This gave us time to clean up and did we ever need that!

Catherine radioed the pilots and soon the two planes set down gently on the lake. Augustus, Catherine, Tim, William and I got on one plane. Maria, Mum, Josh and Thumper got on the other. We flew to a lake in Yellowstone and disembarked. We got onto a waiting bus and headed to a small private airport, where we boarded a Citation jet. When we landed two Tahoe's were waiting for us, and we headed to a dock on the north side of Vancouver. Bobbing next to the dock was perhaps the most beautiful limo tender I had ever seen. Mahogany finish, leather seating and air conditioning. We stepped as eloquently as we could into this amazing craft and off we went. After about thirty minutes of running, we pulled up to a rustic boathouse and slipped inside. The doors shut quietly behind us, and we exited the boat.

Tim led the way as we walked down a wide corridor. It was well lit and pleasant. After about a hundred yards we came to what looked like a solid wall. Tim put his hand up to the wall, and Elle spoke.

"Good afternoon, Tim. I'm afraid I do not recognize one of your party."

"Override. Authorization Beta Zulu, Augustus Helms. Augustus, stand right here while she takes a piece of you." Tim said.

"Okay, mate."

"What floor, Tim?" Elle asked.

"Catherine?"

"Let's go to the kitchen and get some food. I will introduce everyone to the team here." Catherine replied.

"As you wish."

In a moment, we were exiting on the main level. The three people standing in front of us were striking in their own way. A very pretty redhead was in front. She was about five foot six, maybe 140 pounds and very cute. She had a sparkle in her eye that looked oddly familiar. An older woman in her mid-fifties, perhaps, who was a little on the thick side, a younger, fitter version of Mum. She seemed genuinely excited to see us. And a young man, perhaps six foot three inches tall, maybe 225, and obviously very fit. His clothes did little to hide his buff physique. He seemed capable and had a nice relaxed but alert air about him. All in all, it seemed to be a very pleasant group.

"Cynthia. Augustus yelled as he walked briskly towards the younger woman. They embraced as brother and sister.

"Augustus!" the girl squealed as she threw her arms around him.

"Group, let me introduce you to the retreat's team and where we will be for the foreseeable future." Catherine smiled as she introduced everyone. "This young woman who is all over Augustus has good cause. It's his sister, Cynthia. The tall studly looking fellow is Mike. And the lovely house mom is Rebecca. She is a gourmet chef and one of my dearest friends. I'm sure all of you will get to know each other in the next days and weeks to come. Rebecca, is there any food prepared?"

"Yes, we'll have it out in a moment, and everyone can grab a bite, eh." she said.

"Mike, how are the house defenses and the stealth camouflage?" Catherine asked.

"In very good working order, Catherine. We had a sat sweep run of the area just an hour ago and we couldn't detect any signature of any kind in this area. Looks like a mountain full of woods." Mike responded.

"Great. It is so good to be here. It has always been my favorite retreat, and I'm looking forward to showing those of you who have never been here around."

As I looked around the kitchen keeping area, I felt like I was in a beautiful chalet on Whistler Mountain. It had a pleasant warm feeling to it. From the oversized stone fireplaces to the twelve-foot ceilings that were finished in wood. The lighting, the stone floors, everything had a distinct mountain feel and old-world charm. The views out the windows were breathtaking. We were perched on the side of a mountain, cantilevered out beyond the face of the mountain.

"Okay everyone. Cynthia will show you to your rooms. I would like to see everyone in the conference room at about six p.m. We will talk about where we go from here and get an update from William. He should have FEAT rebuilt in a day or two, and for those of you that would like to undergo a treatment we will make it available. It's an irreversible decision. So be sure of your decision." Catherine instructed in a somewhat relaxed tone for the first time in a while.

Chapter 30 – RISK

At precisely six, we filed into the conference room. It held another one of those crazy conference tables with no visible means of support.

"Okay everyone, find a seat and let's get started." Catherine looked around the table. "William, would you like to open?"

"Can I ask a question first?" I queried.

"Sure Todd, go ahead, "she responded.

"What holds the darn tables up?' I asked a little puzzled. The whole group grinned, and I suddenly felt a little foolish.

"Legs, what did you think?" said Tim with a chuckle at my expense.

"Where? I don't see a leg anywhere."

"The same holograph tech we use everywhere hides the legs. he said as he reached under the table and knocked on a wooden sounding object. "We just thought it would be funny to make them look suspended in mid-air." Tim said with a definite smile.

"OK, OK you got me. It's been bugging me from the first day. Everyone have their chuckle at the expense of the new guy." As I chuckled along with them.

"Well ok then, can we get on with it?" Catherine said with a smile and a twinkle in her eye I hadn't seen in a while.

"Sure." William responded. "Let me thank all of you for your sacrifices, and I will be at your disposal from here forward. Each of you that have experienced FEAT will be monitored by your bed and Nimmrod each night. We will use this information to create a database with all of you as the control group. This will help us find out if certain body types or gene groups respond better or slower to FEAT therapy. You are probably noticing that you don't really need to sleep much. I don't have any information at this time about that side effect. We have noticed that most of you go into deep REM sleep in about two minutes and are fully rested in about four hours, give or take. We have also noticed some of you are starting to grow again. We are not sure where that will stop, but we are pretty sure your bodies are just fleshing out to their original growth plate structure. The long and short of it is we need everyone to help us identify the effects of FEAT and help us develop some basic parameters to gage future candidates. Please tell or log into your personal iPads any and all feelings or physical changes you notice. Nothing is too small, so please do not spare the details. Thank you, and I look forward to working with everyone and getting to know all of you on a much more personal level." Potts said with a deep sense of caring for his new friends.

"Thank you, William. We have formed a group we shall call RISK. This stands for responsible individuals seeking knowledge. What we propose is an extraordinary adventure. We will seek out and engage individuals who we think will enhance mankind's journey. Spiritually, scientifically, or from a humanitarian point of view. We do not take this task lightly and we are attempting to discuss all the perils before us. In the days and weeks to come we will develop criteria for candidates and begin to solicit them. We have a lot to talk about and it will be an open forum. Each of the nine people here are part of my most intimate inner circle. I trust each of you with all that I possess and respect every one of your opinions.

Each of you will have a vote on the final selection of each candidate. If seven or more agree, it will be considered a majority vote. William and I think this is the best way to create impartiality. It is a big responsibility, and if anyone does not want to participate, we understand. We have put together a severance package, and we will be able to erase your memory of the last few months with no harm to you. With that said, we hope you decide to join the team and help propel man into the next phase of his journey. Does everyone understand?" Catherine looked around the room, searching each face earnestly. "If you agree, let's have a show of hands." She smiled at the result "I see that it is unanimous. Outstanding choice and may we all stand please. Join hands and let us honor our fallen brothers. Let us go forward and propel man into a new age." Catherine emotionally stated.

In one voice we soberly said. "To the future."

Acknowledgements

To my best friend, Char, who stood by me, coached me, and pushed me to finish. I would not have finished if she had not been there for me. Her many hours of editing, formatting, and grammar correction were invaluable.

Thanks to Bill for editing the rough draft and helping me make a better novel.

And a thanks to my dear friend, Betsy, who gently prodded me without making me feel forced.

About the Author

Michael Savidge uses his boundless imagination to create worlds where he can follow his dreams of endless adventures. For years he was a legend in in own mind, now, setting pen to paper, or more accurately, fingers to keyboard, he puts words to some of his more outrageous thoughts.

Michael grew up as a Navy brat, following his parents all over the world. Hence, his love of all things exotic. With an inquisitive mind, he has explored many different vocations and avocations, from wood wright and home builder to martial arts instructor, to boat captain, to race car driver, to informal studies of physics, art, mathematics, and architecture, just to mention a few. He is a fan of science fiction that follows science, action adventure, and all things erotic.

He can be found in his workshop building furniture for his wife (who commissions endless projects), working on car projects, cruising on his boat, or sitting in front of his computer, dreaming up new adventures to share with the world. He invites you to join him.

Made in the USA
Columbia, SC
09 January 2024

12f57c0b-9221-4415-b613-ee53c9e6cdfcR01